"This book is carried by the literary traditions that the author has taken into her very being, along with an energy fostered by the breaking of cultural and linguistic barriers."
KAN NOZAKI

"In an era where everyone is perhaps too connected, we are forced to consider the importance of the solitude, not loneliness, that is depicted in this novel."
ALISA IWAKAWA, *Gunzo*

"Her knowledge of Taiwanese, Chinese, and Japanese literature, as well as the inevitability of her becoming a writer, is evident in her work, and I look forward to her future career."
MASAAKI TAKEDA, *Shunkan Shincho*

"A striking debut from a young Taiwanese author, which follows the struggles and loneliness of a young woman, from her secret high-school love, to the incident that drastically changes the course of her life, and her eventual journey and escape to Japan."
Kōdansha, Japanese publisher

# SOLO DANCE

# Li Kotomi

# SOLO DANCE

Translated from the Japanese
by Arthur Reiji Morris

WORLD EDITIONS
New York, London, Amsterdam

Published in the USA in 2022 by World Editions LLC, New York
Published in the UK in 2022 by World Editions Ltd., London

World Editions
New York / London / Amsterdam

Printed by Lake Book, USA

World Editions is committed to a sustainable future. Papers
used by World Editions meet the FSC standards of certification.

This book is a work of fiction. Any resemblance to actual
persons, living or dead, or actual events is purely coincidental.

Library of Congress Cataloging in Publication Data is available

ISBN 978-1-64286-114-3

English language translation rights arranged with the author
through New River Literary Ltd.

Twitter: @WorldEdBooks
Facebook: @WorldEditionsInternationalPublishing
Instagram: @WorldEdBooks
YouTube: World Editions
www.worldeditions.org

Book Club Discussion Guides are available on our website.

# CHAPTER 1

Death.

Dying.

She looked through the office window down at the glimmering neon cityscape below as she repeated these words, letting them roll over her tongue.

The words felt good on her lips, their sound gentler than the whispering breeze, softer than any carpet in her dreams.

She didn't have a strong inclination towards death, but she had no attachment to living either. While she still had breath in her lungs, she would do her best in life, yet should it ever reach that point where it was no longer bearable, she would choose death without hesitation.

It wasn't clear to her whether this particular way of thinking was strange or not.

Maybe everyone had the exact same thoughts, but just didn't voice them.

Take the masses of ant-sized people in the city below. How many of them were heading now to their deaths? One heading to fling themselves from a nearby skyscraper, another on their way to leap in front of a passing train. Or one about to get caught in a horrific traffic accident on the way to a fancy restaurant to celebrate their wedding anniversary. In her opinion, life itself amounted to nothing more than pure chance.

"Why can't the human race just hurry up and wipe itself out?"

She remembered those words she had let slip only yesterday. When speaking Japanese, she wasn't always able to control her mouth, and was prone to accidentally voicing her true thoughts.

It was during lunch in the company cafeteria, where Okabe was happily conversing and debating with her and her fellow colleagues. Okabe, two years her senior and a Tokyo University graduate, was tall and slender, with glasses that made his eyes pop like a lemur's; he was intelligent and was well regarded in their department for his mathematical brain. The conversation had found its way to the subject of money. Apparently, Japan had accrued a national debt that was twice the country's GDP, and with the yen weakening towards an unprecedented low, he was suggesting that it was worth judging investments in dollar terms. Her coworkers were listening intently, but she let Okabe's words wash over her. She was twenty-seven and this real-world conversation shouldn't feel so remote, but she couldn't force herself to get interested. There was an insurmountable wall that prevented her from fully engaging with it. All this talk of a decade from now, two decades from now, seemed like the distant future—hundreds if not thousands of years away. A world in which her existence wouldn't make any difference. That was the true representation of her feelings.

Okabe went on at an unfalteringly quick pace. "A nation would sacrifice its own inhabitants in order to prevent the possibility of ruination. Just think of the war," he said, "to pay its debts, the government drained the people of all their financial worth. Although Japan is poor, there are still many who are rich." It was that moment the words slipped out from her lips.

"Why can't the human race just hurry up and wipe itself out?"

She realized her mistake too late. But Okabe had simply glanced at her before saying, "Good question." Not a moment later, the clock announced the end of their lunch break, and she breathed a sigh of relief.

It was a childish and thoughtless remark, but at the same time it was also what she felt. Death leads all of life to an equal end, heals all wounds without bias. It would be a lie to say a small part of her didn't agree with that.

Maybe her way of thinking was in the minority. After all, it was true that she couldn't speak easily of the future the way her colleagues did.

Two years ago, during her induction period, there was a seminar on "life planning." It was a discussion on what kind of life you wanted to lead and what steps you needed to take to get there. The talk eventually moved on to life-threatening risks—accidents, disease—and, with intimidating overtones, suggested risk-management protocols; or, in other words, insurance.

Insurance. If "death" was the word with the most appealing ring to it, then surely "insurance" was the opposite—a concept that was nothing more than the commodification of humanity's innate fear of future uncertainty. And not only this, but its profits rested on the exclusion of those who would benefit from it the most. This inequality never failed to make her stomach turn.

But it seemed like she was the only one who thought this way. Yuka, sitting next to her, cheerfully asked, "Hey, so which plan are you going for?" With aspirations to get married, have two children, and to have purchased her own property before the age of thirty, Yuka earnestly read over the documents they were given about assets under management. Yuka's smile was like a cheerful sunflower, petals in full bloom. Unlike Yuka, to her, the future seemed so distant and fragile, like a bubble, ready to pop at any second. Although a bubble may refract the light in a glorious rainbow, defying gravity as it drifts towards the sky, as soon as it bursts, it vanishes without a trace.

"I'm not going to sign up for any of it," she said simply.

"Really? Are you sure?" Yuka said. The disbelief in Yuka's voice was unmistakeable, but she didn't push the matter any further.

In truth, she wouldn't have been able to join a company-sponsored insurance plan even if she wanted to. To make up for its cheap price, it had an incredibly high barrier to entry. With her history of mental health–related hospitalization and antidepressant prescriptions, she wasn't eligible. In order to avoid any unwanted questions, she didn't dare mention that, though.

Yuka turned instead to her left. "How about you, Erika? Which plan are you going to choose?"

Erika smiled awkwardly and replied, "None, I think. I'm not even sure I can after what happened with my leg. I'll have to talk to my doctor first ..."

"Oh, right. Of course, sorry," Yuka said, awkwardly.

Erika had had an accident during her first year of university which had permanently injured her leg. She knew that she shouldn't give any unwanted sympathy to Erika, but she couldn't help feeling a pang not only of pain but also of pity as she watched her coworker dragging her leg while she walked. After all, she felt a sort of kinship with her. And despite the guilt she felt for feeling this way, she and Erika had an easy friendship.

Erika was an awkward sort and not good at speaking in front of a crowd. The day they were placed in the same department, all new employees had to say a little something about themselves. Erika had stuttered and stammered until she managed to mutter a small "It's a pleasure to work with you" before giving up.

Her own introduction, which happened right afterwards, couldn't have been more different.

"Hello everyone, my name is Chō Norie. I'm from Taiwan, and sorry to ruin your stereotypes but I hate bubble tea and pineapple cake," she'd said, finishing off her bold self-introduction by trying to get a few laughs. Of course, she had refrained from talking about her being a lesbian, about the incident, about her mental illness, about how she had come to Japan in order to escape from Taiwan, about how Norie was a name she'd made up to sound more Japanese.

It was something she had overlooked during their first meeting, but she soon came to notice Erika's mental strength. One occasion that stayed in her mind was when an old man had joined Erika in the company lift, pointed at her leg and said "Must be tough," at which Erika merely smiled and shook her head. "Not at all, there are many far worse off than me," she'd said.

She was amazed at Erika's choice of words, even they were only said to prevent any further questioning. Erika had sounded like she fully accepted the injury and the pain that came with it—but what would happen when Erika encountered something that was simply too painful to bear? Surely people can't just accept every single painful thing that comes their way? Surely it's not so wrong to hide away from a pain you can't accept?

These questions came to her lips as she watched the other her in the glass window, hovering out over the cityscape. Her other self simply opened and closed her mouth, floating silently in the nothingness. She reached out her hand towards the glass and her other self moved closer too, until their palms were touching. The glass spread its coolness through her body. The clouds that floated over the mass of office buildings seemed nothing more than masses of turbid ash. She sighed. The warmth clouded the glass, obscuring her other face.

## CHAPTER 2

No matter how far she traced the threads of memory, she couldn't place the exact moment when that vast darkness had seeped over her, nor identify its source.

She was from a rural area of Changhua, Taiwan, but her family weren't particularly poor, and she hadn't suffered any violence or anything at home. She was raised in the most normal of families—her father sold bikes, her mother was a teacher at the nearby preschool. With two working parents, she had a somewhat affluent youth, always being given books on fairy tales and famous historical figures. A bookworm from a young age, she spent her breaks and time after school working through these books, finger tracing between the Chinese characters and their transcribed sounds—these memories lived with her even now. Her tendency to avoid conversation led her classmates and teachers to look at her with suspicion.

"I'm a little worried about Yingmei. She always has this frown on her face," her homeroom teacher said once, unaware that she was listening from outside the door. Yingmei—she who greets the plum blossoms—was her given name, chosen because of her January birthday.

From the day that she became aware of the world around her, she had the faint realization she was different to her peers. Every time she read another fairy tale where the princess and prince find each other she felt strongly that something wasn't quite right with the story. Rather than imagining herself as one of these passive princesses, she imagined herself as Dorothy, on an exciting adventure with the beautiful Good Witch of the North. The way she felt was clearly different from the other kids around her.

It was when she moved up to the fourth grade and the classes were shuffled around that she met Shi Danchen and finally understood the meaning behind this constant, faint unease. Danchen, so pale, always had a vague expression, her emotions guarded, her movements so helpless that it seemed she might vanish into thin air at any moment. The black pupils of her eyes were cast in an almost indigo shimmer, bringing to mind the image of a quiet lake illuminated by the moon. Even when Danchen would appear in her dreams many decades later, although her features grew more unclear with every passing year, those eyes would always remain fresh in her memory.

She was drawn to Danchen the moment she saw those eyes. Though she was too young to understand the meaning of love in even its most basic sense, she knew that squirming, roiling wave of emotion in her chest was the same one felt between those fairy-tale princes and princesses.

She spent her days watching Danchen but never managed to exchange a word with her.

It was on an autumn day a year later, during the ceremony to celebrate moving up into fifth grade, that their teacher announced Danchen's death. Danchen had been riding on the back of her mother's motorcycle on the way to a piano lesson during the summer holidays when she and her mother collided with a dump truck carrying stone. The teacher ordered a three-minute silence for the class, and as her fellow students quieted down, her own mind was racing. Just where would Danchen go now that she was dead? And what about her body? She tried to imagine Danchen's pale, near-blue face in eternal rest.

A few days later, their teacher took the whole class to offer up incense at the hospital. A black-and-white photograph of Danchen hung at the end of the corridor leading to the mortuary, and the students lined themselves up in two rows in silence as the teacher offered up the incense on their behalf. She stared up at Danchen's photograph and Danchen stared back with a soft and melancholic smile on her lips. Danchen was beautiful. She let out a sigh.

"I wish we could see Danchen again," her classmate said after school.

"Right? I mean, I'd love to see her again, even if it's just her dead body."

It was through the glares of her classmates,

stood together in a circle, that she realized her blunder. Looking back on that moment, she saw how insensitive her remark was, but at the time she was simply stating what was on her mind. She wasn't yet old enough to know she shouldn't talk about death, and any idea of what a horrific state a body might be in after being crushed by a dump truck was beyond her wildest imagination. It didn't matter whether she was alive or dead—to her, Danchen was simply beautiful.

Her memories of Danchen froze that day, never to be revised. Time would never move again for Danchen. But for her, time marched forward regardless.

She saw Danchen in a dream. She knew it was a dream the instant it began, even from inside it. Danchen still had the same peaceful yet melancholic smile on her lips, and those eyes, basked in sorrow, were staring straight into her soul. *Ah, what sadness*, she thought. But she didn't know where this sadness came from. Was this Danchen's sadness, or was it her own? It was then that she noticed Danchen was fading further away. No, that wasn't it. Danchen wasn't moving away—she was. She and Danchen were standing in a river, yet as she was herself pushed further away by the current, Danchen stayed there quietly, watching her struggle in the water.

She awoke to a violent jolt and sounds of chaos from all around. The very heavens and earth were shaking. Danchen was gone. Outside, the night was still dark, the only source of light came from the faint glow of her room's security light. The paintings on her wall were on the floor. Her wooden bookcase had toppled over, spilling its contents, history books and world literature. She heard glass smashing. A distant shriek. The bustling of her neighbours. The wail of an ambulance. *How much better would it be if the world ended, right here and now*, she thought, her mind still foggy. Soon the security light blinked out. She closed her eyes. A faint moisture tickled her eyelids. Danchen's face floated again in the darkness.

When she opened her eyes, she was being carried by her father. Her two-year-old brother was in her mother's arms. They were outside the house. Dawn had not yet broken.

In the faint ochre glow of the streetlamps, she could make out the silhouettes of her neighbours. The clamour showed no sign of quietening. Children were crying—a boy, a girl. The sound of the radio. She tilted her head back and stared up at the night sky. The moon gave off a gentle glow, almost full, except for a sliver of darkness.

It was then that she finally understood: *I'll never see Danchen again.*

## CHAPTER 3

"So, was that when you realized, Xiaohui? That you only liked women?"

This was Sho's first reaction when she laid bare the events of the night of that great earthquake and her memories of Danchen.

The two of them were in Lilith, a bar in Shinjuku's Ni-chōme area. Xiaohui—from her Chinese name, Jihui—was her username for Chinese LGBT websites, and Rie—from the Japanese version of her name, Norie— was for Japanese ones.

"Not 'only' women, just that I liked women," she said, correcting Sho.

Sho was also from Taiwan, this nickname being a play on her real name—her name was Li Shurou, and the Chinese character for *shu* was pronounced *sho* in Japanese. Her name could have been made into a typical

Chinese nickname by adding *xiao* to it, but unfortunately Xiaoshu sounded the same as "old man," so Sho tended to avoid it. She and Sho were the same age, but unlike her, Sho hadn't come to Japan immediately after university and had worked in Taiwan for a few years instead. This was still only her second year in Japan and she was attending language school while also trying to find a job. In her early days here, Sho had posted a thread on a Taiwanese lesbian forum titled "Looking for like-minded friends in Tokyo!" which is how the two of them met.

"Same difference, right?"

"No way. When you say 'only' it makes it sound like a negative thing."

"You really do sweat the small stuff," Sho said with a smirk before taking a sip of her golden beer. "That pickiness is very Japanese of you."

"Excuse me, I'm not at all picky, thank you. I'm just being precise in my wording," she laughed back.

Sho's laid-back, relaxed, and almost sloppy attitude was completely at odds with her own tendency to overthink the smallest things. Sho's careless behaviour was often a source of frustration and despair for her, but she always felt better when they were together.

Ni-chōme was lively on a Friday night, and with the cooler days ahead as September came to a close, Tokyo was in the perfect temperate zone between its muggy summers and skin-bitingly cold winters. It was eleven o'clock and the low thump-thump of club music reverberated from the bars and venues nearby, numerous gay couples walked the streets side by side, and long queues of eager customers were waiting to enter the popular spots.

In Lilith, too, upbeat music was playing out over the speakers, and twenty to thirty other customers were crammed into the small room. They were a number of ages—from twentysomethings to those in their forties—and although the majority were Japanese, there were also other Chinese speakers as well as a few white women chatting together in English. Lilith was essentially a women-only bar, but there were a large number of customers who looked androgynous. In the corner, a young woman, probably a university student, with long, straight black hair was getting ready to sing karaoke. The up-tempo Western music that had been playing faded out as the first melodies of Takako Matsu's Japanese cover of "Let It Go" began to play.

"You complain about Japanese people, so why did you come to Japan in the first place?" she asked Sho.

Japanese people had asked her this tedious question a million times before, but now she was redirecting it at Sho. She had been wondering why Sho continued to stay in Japan for a while now. Although other countries were beginning to acknowledge the existence of an LGBT community in recent years, Japan still lived up to its negative reputation of being a "queer desert." Not only that, on a personal level Sho was still finding it hard to integrate into Japanese society despite having lived in Tokyo for a year and a half already. Whenever they met, she always had some gripe—that Japanese people were too stubborn, too fussy, always focusing on petty little details, too conformist and group-minded.

"I didn't really think about it too much. A friend asked me to come, so I did."

"What? As if. Give me a proper answer."

Sho never talked about her personal life with any seriousness and had a tendency to avoid answering questions. She let out a frustrated sigh and furrowed her brow in thought before finally answering.

"You wouldn't know unless you've had a job there, but I couldn't see a future for myself in Taiwan. I couldn't see myself having any dreams, let alone making them come true. All I was doing was joining the sea of motorbikes as I headed to work, working myself to the bone, earning enough not to die of starvation, and just about making it through life."

Sho took another swig of beer. Waiting for Sho to continue, she raised her glass of Kahlúa and milk to her lips. In the corner, the student had reached the chorus of "Let It Go." Sho went on, "Even now, whenever I think of the sky in Taipei, all I can see in my head is a suffocating mass of grey clouds. One day, on the way to work, I was waiting at the traffic lights when I looked up and thought: Do I really have to spend the next two or three decades looking up at this same sky?"

Sho's eyes glittered with both the fear of a lifeless, unchanging future and the desire to effect some change.

"As I waited for the light to turn green, I looked over at the street corner and saw a Yoshinoya restaurant. And I thought, I know, I'll go to Japan. I told the girl I was dating at the time and, naturally, she flipped out. She cried buckets, holding on to me as she begged me not to leave her. She almost convinced me—I mean, I had no money, I couldn't even speak Japanese. But my mind was set. It was as if the desire to leave that island for somewhere new had planted its roots in my heart and wouldn't let go. I broke up with her, quit my job, borrowed some money, left, and here we are today."

Sho gave a bitter smile as she drained her glass before immediately ordering another. Finished with her Kahlúa and milk, she ordered a cassis and orange juice. Depending on how you looked at it, Sho's resolute decision could seem spur-of-the-moment and irresponsible, but it also said something about her individuality, her own inherent freedoms, her refusal to bow down to the logic of others. In all honesty, she was jealous of that side of Sho. Although she herself had made a number of decisions in her life up till now, they weren't the culmination of an inherent desire to be free, merely the most logical solution at a given juncture. In many ways, it felt as if she were some kind of puppet, being pulled towards whatever came next by some unknown force.

The last notes of "Let It Go" faded out, and the bar erupted into applause. Sho grabbed the karaoke remote and reserved a song for herself, "The Thorn Bird," by the Taiwanese group F.I.R. It was typical of Sho to pointedly choose a Chinese song despite the majority of the bar being Japanese, and she admired this confident side to her.

As the song began, the atmosphere of the bar immediately soured, but Sho began to sing, a huge smile on her lips, with no regard for anyone else's opinion. She sat there, listening to her friend belt out the words.

*Just like the thorn bird's destiny*
*Tragedy and bravery entwined*
*Let's choose to bloom a glittering end*
*In exchange for our lives*

## CHAPTER 4

The great earthquake of September 21, 1999, that shook Taiwan to its core also took away part of her soul.

Whenever she closed her eyes, Danchen's face would silently appear before her. Whenever she sank into the world of dreams, Danchen's faint smile would be floating in the dark. Even when she was awake and outside, the white flowers that bloomed at the end of the road had the same sweet scent as Danchen—the smell of death; the last vestiges of the deceased. The truth of Danchen's death thrust before her, she clung as best she could to her memories. She felt that as long as she was able to do so, then the sky would be able to remain blue, the world would be able to remain full of colour.

Yet, as the monsoon season set in, her

memories started to fade. Danchen's face appeared now only as a fuzzy silhouette. Apart from those two mournful eyes, Danchen's face became nothing more than a blur of dust, threatening to blow away with a sudden gust of wind. Soon that dust too lost its colour, turning into nothing more than lifeless ash. Not long after, the world around her followed, painted over in a dull monochrome.

She couldn't remember when the crying started, when it became just another part of her everyday routine, as regular as dinner. Tears would well out of her eyes without warning. She couldn't focus on her homework or her studies, and her grades plummeted—taking her from top of the class straight down to the bottom. After her first period came, Danchen started to appear in her dreams as a bloodied corpse and she would awake to find herself screaming. When her parents went out, they would return to find her with a red marker pen in hand, the walls covered in scribbles, or with a Boy Scouts' rope coiled around her neck. Horrified by her strange behaviour, they sought help from any source they could find.

They were scared that maybe their daughter's soul had slipped from her body due to the shock of the earthquake and so they first took her to a temple. They performed purification rites to remedy her condition, forcing her to drink a mixture of burned prayer papers and water. But seeing no change, her parents next decided to seek the aid of Western science, and she began counselling at a youth mental health centre.

These fortnightly counselling sessions soon became intolerable, as the counselling room would remind her of the stark mortuary. *They could never possibly understand my pain*, she thought, and so she spent each session in silence. *I loved Danchen, but now Danchen is gone.* She didn't know what she could possibly do to make herself say these words out loud. Her counsellor would try to pry into her heart, searching for the cause of her abnormality, and yet the questions that came out of his mouth were laughably off the mark. Her parents tried to offer some direction, but comments like "she started acting like this after the earthquake" only served to mislead and cause the counsellor to think that her behaviour was due to the traumatic experience of the quake.

Not one person even considered it might be about Danchen. To begin with, the number of people who truly worried about her were so few. Before all this, she had been a quiet child who spent her breaks and time between lessons sitting alone reading at her desk. She never went out to play with her classmates, and she always walked home alone. She often thought that the only reason she never got bullied was because her presence was too negligible to warrant it.

Along came the turn of the century, and the next two years passed by in a flash, as if someone had pressed the fast-forward button on her life. She had few memories of that time, and found herself finishing elementary school at the bottom of her class. She didn't bother to attend the school's graduation ceremony, but still they posted her out a commemorative album, as if to force her to accept the fact that her elementary school life was over. She decided to open it one July afternoon, the hot air buzzing with a cacophony of cicada cries, and flicked through its matte pages, only six of its hundred-plus pages dedicated to her class. Apart from the obligatory school photos, she was only in one other photo. She stared at the group of her classmates alongside her, struggling to put names to those faces she had known so well. It was hard to believe that they had been together for three whole years.

A photo of Danchen and three other students caused the breath to stop in her throat. They were in their classroom, Danchen sitting at the organ and the other students standing around it. And all four pairs of eyes were staring at her. This wasn't just because they were looking at the camera; she remembered now—she was the one who had taken this photo.

It was during a music lesson in fourth grade. Their teacher had found out that Danchen could play the piano and so asked her to play a piece for the class. They only had an organ in the music room, but still Danchen's skillful playing captured her heart, if not the hearts of the entire class. During break time afterwards, one of her classmates happened to have a camera and so asked Danchen if it was all right to take a photo to remember the day by. Two others wanted to be in it as well, so they agreed the four of them should be in the photograph. The group asked her to take it, with no reason other than she had been sitting closest to the organ.

If her memory served her correctly, Danchen played a movement from Mozart's Requiem that day. She had read about Mozart long ago and the stories surrounding the Requiem. Apparently, it was an unfinished work which had been commissioned by a mysterious man not long before Mozart passed away. The legend went that this man was the Grim Reaper. Aware of Mozart's imminent death, he had come to request Mozart to write a requiem for himself.

Why did Danchen choose to play this piece that day? Perhaps Danchen had chosen it because she could sense something bad would befall her soon.

As she stared at the photograph, she felt streaks of warmth running down her cheeks. *Crying again*, she thought, wiping away the tears, *stupid illness*—and as this thought ran across her mind, she was struck by a strange feeling. An unfamiliar force was bubbling from the depths of her heart, suddenly swallowing her emotions whole. She wept. Not her usual sucking sobs, but great wailing cries. She buried her face in her bed sheets, unfazed that they gradually grew soaked by those unrelenting tears.

If the Requiem was Mozart's parting gift to himself, something that he could bring with him to the other side, then what about Danchen? Had she managed to take something with her? She doubted it. After all, Danchen's death had been too swift to allow her to prepare anything to bring with her to that other realm. These thoughts came over her as she wept. If that was the case, then she wanted to create something for Danchen and ease her soul. She was no musician, so she couldn't write any music: all she had were words.

She wasn't sure how long she had been crying—one hour, two? Having exhausted her tears, she stood up and sat at her desk, pulled out a paper and pen, and began to write.

It was a poem containing her thoughts to Danchen and her feelings upon her passing.

於是有天我會想起, 想起那：
　　在開始前便已結束的故事
　　未曾碰觸便已失溫的側臉
　　不及掬起便已流乾的血液
大河奔向海洋, 群鳥回歸山林
流光殞墜, 餘下一縷鎮魂的琴音

*One day I will remember*
*Your story that ended before it began*
*Your face that lost all warmth before I could*
　　*touch it*
*Your hardened blood that I failed to scoop into*
　　*my hands*
*Just as the river runs towards the sea, the*
　　*birds flock to the forest*
*Light flows onward; the way you left behind a*
　　*pacifying melody for your soul*

Without her noticing, the sun was beginning to set and the cicadas' cries had ceased, swathing her room in silence. The sun was casting a blood-red glow through the window as her shadow grew longer. The shadow was pitch black. Like Danchen's eyes. She realized in that moment that in order to keep living she needed to keep looking at and keep chasing this colour.

It was strange how writing about death had allowed her to keep living.

## CHAPTER 5

If she hadn't fallen in love with Danchen, then maybe she would never have begun to write. If she'd never discovered the world of literature, then maybe she would never have encountered Qiu Miaojin's writing. If she'd never read Qiu Miaojin, then she would never have found out about Qiu's love for Haruki Murakami and Osamu Dazai. If she'd never read these writers and grown interested in Japanese literature, then perhaps she would never have left Taiwan to start a new life in Japan. Her existence felt like a string of coincidental moments, all of which led to now.

But no matter how coincidental, the fact of the matter was that she was here in Tokyo, a place that Qiu had once visited herself. She was in junior high school when she discovered Qiu, but now here she was, in the blink of an eye aged twenty-seven, and she had outlived her.

Moments before piercing her heart with that cold knife and causing that flower of blood to blossom in the Paris of 1995, aged only twenty-six, Qiu Miaojin had telephoned her friend Lai Hsiang-yin, who was at the time living in Tokyo. Upon telling Lai Hsiang-yin what to do with her manuscripts after she was gone, Qiu hung up. In that moment, the line tying them together was severed, as was the thread tying Qiu to the world of the living, a gossamer filament that snapped so suddenly.

While Qiu's works were full of a suffocatingly self-destructive despair, Qiu herself was like a star, both figuratively and literally, viewed as a boundless fountain of life by those around her. A psychology graduate, she knew what made people work, and even practised as a counsellor. "I have been given so much by the world, by so many people, yet how pathetic I am, that I cannot even allow myself to continue living in slightly less pain than I am now," Qiu wrote in *Last Words from Montmartre*, the final work she penned before she died. Although the book can be read as a suicide note, it was never intended to be so. As Qiu stood on the precipice overlooking death, Lai Hsiang-yin tried to save her. Qiu tried to force herself to keep on living by writing about death, but despite her many struggles, her efforts were in vain. Whether her death was inevitable or not, no one knows.

It was a blustery Saturday in February, one month after her twenty-seventh birthday, and she was heading towards a lesbian club night in Omotesandō. To dull her pain, she longed for deafening music, booze, and a space where she could dance as wildly as she wanted.

Sho was with her, along with Sophia, a Taiwanese woman, and Aki, who was Japanese. Of course, both names were their online usernames. At eleven thirty, there were few cars on the road and most people were heading to the station, yet the club still had a large queue snaking out from the entrance.

The queue was moving, but slowly; after half an hour they still couldn't see the entrance. Thirty minutes in the biting cold was starting to take its toll and their hand warmers had lost all but residual heat. As the four of them jogged on the spot for warmth, she pointed over at the nearby Family Mart. "How about I buy something for us while we wait?" she suggested, receiving orders of hot coffee, hot cocoa, and extra hand warmers.

She left the crowd and crossed the street to the convenience store. The array of items in her arms, she was about to head for the till when a familiar voice called from behind, "Is that you, Norie?" She spun round—it was Erika and Okabe.

She couldn't process seeing Erika here of all places, let alone with Okabe. She glanced down at their hands clasped together and worked out the situation on the spot.

"Hey, Erika! What a coincidence. What are you doing here? Hello, Okabe," she said, keeping her expression calm. She and Okabe were in the same division, and although Erika was in a different one, they all belonged to the same department and so worked on the same floor. She had seen them talking a number of times, so it wasn't too much of a surprise for them to be together now.

"Takeshi and I were just out for dinner," Erika said, the colour rushing to her cheeks. She realized her mistake a moment later: she had used Okabe's first name. Erika corrected herself, appearing more awkward than before: "I mean, Okabe, of course ... So, what about you, Norie? What are you doing here this late? Do you live nearby?"

"No way. I'm way too poor to live around Omotesandō. Some friends from Taiwan invited me out drinking nearby. It's looking to be an all-nighter so I thought I'd grab some supplies," she said, somewhere between the truth and a lie.

"Wow, that's amazing. You're so international," Erika said.

She puzzled at Erika's words. What was international about her going drinking with someone else from Taiwan? And why was Erika using the word "international" as if it were meant to be a compliment?

She avoided responding to this and engaged in further small talk for a little while —I hope it gets warmer soon, where did you go over New Year's, work sure is tough lately.

Okabe asked her about the upcoming Taiwanese presidential election, so she explained the histories of the Democratic Progressive Party and the Kuomintang, aka the Chinese Nationalist Party, and how the latter were losing support among young voters and were expected to lose the election. The DPP weren't a pro-Chinese party, so Taiwanese-Japanese relations would grow stronger if they came into power. But, if this *were* to happen, it would be foolish for the people to ignore China's influence in Taiwan. And so she went on, seeming more like she was interviewing for a job in international relations than having a conversation with friends.

They spoke for about ten minutes before Erika and Okabe made to go. Just as they were leaving, Erika turned and said, with a longing glint in her smile, "I sometimes feel really jealous of you, Norie. You're always so full of energy, so confident in yourself. Oh, and I haven't told anyone about me and Okabe, so keep it a secret at the office, okay?"

Okabe guided Erika along as they left the store, before hopping into a silver car and speeding off into the night.

Erika was jealous of her? Erika's words reverberated in her heart and each time she heard their echo, her chest tightened. She clenched her teeth and pushed down the feeling of helplessness that kept rising within. No matter how loud the music, how strong the alcohol, that hole in her heart still wouldn't close. She could hear the wind whistling through it. No matter how deep she plunged her memories, they would come bubbling back up to confront her.

She was jealous of Erika.

Erika knew nothing about her. Erika didn't know about her past or sexuality, let alone the dirty look Kaori had thrown at her before dumping her only a month ago.

# CHAPTER 6

She was in high school when she first dated someone she liked.

With her appalling results at elementary school and her parents' worries about her mental health, they decided not to send her to a junior high school in the city but one closer to their home.

Many schools in the countryside were keen to raise their standing and the only way to do so was to produce students with good grades who could go on to study at highly renowned senior high schools. To achieve this, they wouldn't hesitate to use any inhumane method available. First graders were expected to turn up at school at 7 a.m. and leave at five thirty. In the second year, Saturday schooling was introduced, and in the third they were forced to do self-study until nine thirty at night. There were no clubs, no field trips, and, naturally, dating wasn't permitted. During the periods listed as Music, Home Economics, Art, and Homeroom, the students were instead forced to study Chinese, English, Maths, and Science. Corporal punishment and bullying from the teachers were an everyday occurrence, and should your grades be "bad"—in other words anything lower than 90%—they would rap your knuckles with the cane. In this way, the school would create students who could get into well-respected high schools by any means necessary, and each year a large banner would be draped by the school entrance stating, *Congratulations to the* X *students who got into* Y *High School!* The lucky few would be fawned over for a short while, but soon they would be forgotten as the next year rolled around. The Taiwanese education system was often likened to a canning factory, and her school in particular stuffed its students uniformly full of knowledge that would evaporate before long; the students themselves were regarded as nothing more than disposable tools.

Despite such an environment, her years at this school were far healthier than her final years at elementary school. Since discovering writing, her symptoms had subsided, and six months later she stopped attending counselling. She had been a good student beforehand, and soon enough her grades climbed back up to the top ranks of her class, which granted her the leeway to spend more of her time on writing without being told off. At first, she was only able to write short poems regarding death, but the more she wrote, the more diversified her works became, and she succeeded in having a piece published in a literary magazine for young writers.

Despite the upturn in her mental state, she had always been a solitary child, and she began to think of this isolation as a necessary element for writing. Whether it was on proper manuscript paper or in the margins of a textbook, whenever she began to write the hubbub surrounding her faded to a distant echo. The fact that few people tried to talk to her anyway and that talking to anyone else was too much effort gave her a sense of solitude and outsideness that felt good. After all, she sensed that same kind of solitude in the works of many authors she admired: Sanmao, Qiu Miaojin, Ryūnosuke Akutagawa, Osamu Dazai, and Yukio Mishima. She only found out later another fact about all these authors—that they had all ended their lives by their own hand—and this only served to further her connection with their works, in particular Qiu, whose writing she devoured. When she finally started to read Haruki Murakami, her dissatisfaction at reading his works in translation led her to study Japanese to read them in the original language. There was little in her life outside of study and literature, and she was forced to continue hiding her sexuality—luckily with no misfortunes along the way—but her hard work allowed her to get into the prestigious Taichung Girls' Senior High School. She left her home in the countryside and began living on her own in the city.

It was among that sea of green school shirts that she met Yang Haoxue—a girl swathed in an aura of intelligence whose calm expression betrayed neither happiness nor anger.

They had both joined the school's magazine club, where their work was to research and write articles for its regular issues as well as hold writing competitions. At first, she found Haoxue difficult to get along with. Haoxue was tall, with an imposing air and beautiful features, which gave her the impression of being difficult to approach, and on top of this Haoxue's emotions were hard to read and made her feel uncomfortable. There was no reason for them to talk throughout their first year at senior high, and so the year went by with them working on the school magazine in silence in the same room, their only small talk regarding their work.

The day this changed was in December during their second year. It was the school sports day, and she had snuck out of the cheering crowds to seek refuge in the library. She wasn't particularly sporty, and due to the change of classes in September as the students chose whether to focus on arts or science, she was finding it hard to get along with her new classmates.

Haoxue was in the library's reading room.

She was in a chair by the window, quietly reading a book. The gentle winter light was pouring in through the window, basking Haoxue in a golden glow. The library was empty aside from them, and as she looked at her, Haoxue seemed like she was sitting alone, separate from the world. Motes of dust caught the light, like solidified sunlight. It was almost as if she'd stepped into a painting.

Intrigued by what Haoxue was reading, she approached slowly, one step at a time, so as not to shatter Haoxue's solemn air. It was just as the title was close enough to read that Haoxue noticed her presence and looked up. It was Haoxue who broke those few seconds of silence between them.

"Hello there, I didn't realize you had come too."

Haoxue's words struck her heart. *She's looking at me—she's noticed me.*

Those words were a famous line from Eileen Chang's "Love." "Love" was a short work, only a few hundred words long, yet it managed to contain an inexplicable amount of pain within it. She had been reading a lot of Eileen Chang recently, and was particularly drawn to "Love." The fact that Haoxue chose this line must mean she had been watching her.

"I hope happiness and health await you," she said quietly.

Haoxue was reading *Last Words from Montmartre*—and this was its last line.

Haoxue stared at her for a second before breaking into a smile. The frozen space between them thawed as they found common ground.

From that day onward, Yang Haoxue became Xiaoxue to her—meaning "Little Snow." This was a nickname reserved for her and her alone. Although they didn't share any classes, Xiaoxue would always come to her classroom during break times. Her classmates didn't make any comments or fuss upon seeing the two of them together. As in other girls' schools, there was an unspoken rule—whether you noticed two classmates were dating or you spotted them kissing in the bathroom or whatever, you kept it to yourself.

"It seems that our days of being called Lazi are over," Xiaoxue said one day.

"Seems so. I guess time can change everything," she replied.

*Maybe, just maybe, I've been blessed with luck,* she thought. After all, unlike Qiu Miaojin, who suffered through the nineties, she was fortunate enough to be able to enjoy her youth at the turn of the century. "Lazi" was the name of the protagonist of Qiu's *Notes of a Crocodile*; the character was said to be a representation of Qiu herself and the suffering she endured due to her sexuality. After Qiu died, *Notes of a Crocodile* became a bestseller, and along with its success, "Lazi" became a slang term for lesbians in Taiwan.

Qiu was often a topic of conversation between the two of them.

"Yingmei, you were born in the same place as Qiu Miaojin, weren't you?" Xiaoxue asked one day, as if the thought had come to her in that moment.

Both she and Qiu were from Changhua, while Xiaoxue was born and raised in Taichung. She'd never been to Xiaoxue's house as they were worried her parents would find out about their relationship. Instead, their dates took them to the bustling parts of Yizhong, to art galleries, to museums, but often to her apartment. It was a small room, only fifteen square metres, without facilities—the toilet and shower were communal—and contained a grimy wardrobe, an old single bed, and a crack-covered wooden desk and chair, all of which had come with the flat. The window faced the main road, yet despite the blaring sounds of traffic during rush hour and the grime from car exhausts that settled on the glass, they enjoyed their time alone in this squalid room. They read their favourite poems to each other, read each other's work, and shared ideas and suggestions, or simply did nothing but enjoy idle conversation.

"Yeah, and who knows, maybe I'll die at twenty-six, too, just like her."

"If you were set on dying, I wouldn't stop you," Xiaoxue said.

"So, you wouldn't mind if I died?"

"Of course I'd mind, but if that's what you really, truly wanted, I wouldn't stop you, Yingmei. I mean, it would be awfully presumptuous of me to decide your life for you."

"Would you mourn me?"

"I would follow you."

"You can't. I couldn't stand it if you died."

"Then keep on living. Let's both keep on living until we're seventy-year-old grannies. Then we can find a beautiful cliff and throw ourselves into the sea from it."

"You're overestimating how much an old granny can climb, you know," she said, but despite the joke, she didn't think Xiaoxue's idea was all that bad. She was seventeen now, and the idea of living out the next fifty-odd years didn't seem too unpleasant if she would be with Xiaoxue. She thought of the years ahead, her mind's eye untainted by worries about what society would think or the fact that she wouldn't be able to marry someone she loved.

"But if we were to die," Xiaoxue went on, "wouldn't you first want to bloom beautifully? For a moment before dying? You know, like the thorn bird."

"What's that?"

"You really don't know?" Xiaoxue's face

was held in an expression of surprise. "I thought you of all people would know about the legend of the thorn bird, Yingmei."

"Why do you say that?"

"Because everything you write, it's covered in the haze of death, if you get what I mean. I can always feel death at the heart of your writing. So many of your stories have the protagonist being saved through death, right?"

Xiaoxue was always serious when talking about her writing. It felt as if she could see right through her. It made her feel embarrassed. Xiaoxue went on without waiting for an answer.

"Not only that, don't you think Qiu Miaojin's life was a little like the thorn bird's?"

"Like I said, I don't know what this thorn bird is. Fill me in already."

"Well, I only learnt about it through F.I.R.'s latest album, to be honest."

Xiaoxue pulled out her phone and connected it to some cheap speakers. The slow melody that flowed leisurely out from the speakers brought to mind a distant, exotic country. Or perhaps stretching golden sands underneath an azure sky, or maybe a stately cathedral, cast in shadow, weathered down by the sands of time.

"The thorn bird is this bird that only sings once in its life, ever. From the day it flies the nest, it spends its life in search of a tree covered in sharp thorns. One day it finally finds this tree, and seeking its deadliest and sharpest thorn, it flies straight towards it to take its life. However, in the last moments before it dies, it sings a beautiful song that transcends the pain of dying. This bird's voice is more beautiful than any other, so much so that even God is enraptured by it. That's the legend of the thorn bird."

"So, in exchange for its life, it gives the world the most beautiful song," she murmured to herself.

This was the first time she had heard of this legend. A part of her could see the logic—maybe one's life is a small price to pay to create something of immense beauty. Xiaoxue was right—Qiu transformed the pain of her existence into art, just like the thorn bird, before she departed from this life leaving behind *Last Words from Montmartre* and *Notes of a Crocodile*, works that would influence the world long after she had gone.

She expressed this to Xiaoxue, who nodded. "Exactly. I think you could even go so far as to say that these works gave meaning to her death. I mean, if not, it's just a bit tragic."

She cast her thoughts to Danchen. If that was the case, then what meaning did Danchen's death hold?

She kept this thought to herself, trapped within her head, and replied, "All right, then neither of us is allowed to die until we find a meaning to our lives."

Xiaoxue's face broke out in a grin. The light from the fading sun cast her features in an otherworldly colour, not quite red, not quite purple.

"That's a promise."

Xiaoxue approached her and grasped her hand tightly in her own. Eyes closed, their lips touched, almost of their own accord. A sweetness wafted from Xiaoxue—a smell that reminded her of the proud blooming of innumerable flowers in spring, filled with the vitality of life. She had never felt as alive as she did now. She let Xiaoxue's scent and the energy it carried flow into her. As if sipping from the eternal spring of life, she stopped thinking and allowed her body to do the rest.

## CHAPTER 7

Perhaps if what happened hadn't happened, she would still be with Xiaoxue now. Or maybe not, who knows? They were young then, at that age where you want to find meaning in everything. But, in this world, sometimes things simply happen for no reason at all.

Being dumped by Kaori was meaningless. Going to the club last night to soothe the pain of being dumped was meaningless, too. It was true that while she was there, drink in hand, moving her body in time with the music, her worries had floated to the heavens. She stared around the room full of women and was able to convince herself that being dumped by one person wasn't really that big a deal in the grand scheme of things. However, as the next day came along, leaving her incapacitated in bed with a hangover, she was plunged into a deeper despair than the night before. The lurking fear in her chest that the world had given up on her came welling up and out through her eyes as tears. She had at one time believed she was free from the shackles of her past, but Kaori had proved what a misunderstanding that was.

*Wallow in your sorrows all you like today, but cheer up by tomorrow.*

Even in the depths of her despair, there was another more rational version of herself that looked down upon the wailing, emotional her and offered cool-headed advice. It was thanks to this version of herself that she never gave herself completely over to despair, that she was able to at least present herself as a functional human being in front of others.

Nevertheless, a directionless anger welled up within her. *Why do I have to feel this way? I've lived my life trying not to do anything wrong, trying not to hurt anyone, trying to suppress this gnawing, squirming sadness within my soul. So why do I have to deal with this shit?*

As these thoughts crossed her mind, a

sense of relief washed over her: while she still felt anger, she could continue to live. The pain of existence was still within the boundaries of the bearable. Should the day come where even her anger should dull utterly into sorrow, it would be then that she would take her life.

She took a double dosage of antidepressants before returning to bed. Soon her heart began to slow as she calmed down, and by work the next day she had retrieved a sense of normalcy again. During lunch she bumped into Erika, whose cheeks flushed upon spotting her; the two of them decided to eat together.

"You haven't told anyone, have you? About Take—about Okabe," Erika said.

She had tried her best not to broach the topic of Okabe, but Erika had dived into the matter of her own free will.

"Of course not. Do I look like a gossip?" she said with a smile. She went on, finding some joy in making Erika uncomfortable. "So, spill the details. How long have you been seeing each other?"

Erika's already flushed cheeks grew a

deeper shade of scarlet. She lowered her head as she replied, "Since October last year. So, I mean, it's only been four months since we started dating, but we're going to go see his parents in Nagano in May already, during Golden Week."

"Meeting the in-laws. Sounds like a big step."

Erika's face somehow grew a deeper shade of red, yet a trace of a smile played on her lips. She nodded quietly. "If things go well, Okabe will be coming to see my parents in August, when we have time off for Obon." Erika's family were from Hokkaidō, so she was living in Tokyo on her own.

"Bet you're looking forward to that."

"I am, but, well, I'm a bit nervous, too." Erika's earlier smile and excitement seemed to lose their colour as her expression clouded over. "You see, Okabe's from a farming family, and his parents are landowners, pretty traditional ones at that. Fortunately, Okabe's the youngest of three and his two older brothers are already married. But apparently, both of their wives have quit their jobs and agreed to help carry on the family business."

This was news to her. Okabe was always going on about the latest international developments or world economics, so it came as a surprise to learn he was from such a traditional family.

"Have you thought about marriage yet?"

Erika gave a shy nod.

"And you're scared that if you choose to continue working it'll become awkward and they'll talk about you behind your back?"

Erika nodded again, before answering, "There are other things, too. My leg's the way it is, and, well, I'm not even sure if Okabe's family would accept someone like me. Okabe graduated from Tokyo University—he's their pride and joy. What if they don't think I'm good enough for him?"

Marriage was something that didn't concern her, yet she could see how sincerely Erika was worrying over it.

"Erika, you're super clever. You got into this company on your own merits, didn't you? I doubt they'll say a bad word about you. But more importantly, what about what you want, Erika? Do you want to keep working?"

"Yes, I think so. But," Erika hesitated,

before going on, "Norie, what would you do if you were me? What would you do if you got married and were asked to quit your job for the family?"

"I'd keep working, obviously. I can't imagine quitting my job just because I got married. It's the twenty-first century, for crying out loud."

Erika fell into a deep silence. She worried that perhaps she'd gone too far and had upset Erika. The reason she couldn't imagine what her life would be like if she got married was largely because marriage simply was not possible for her. But perhaps a softer choice of words would have been less harsh on Erika. The two of them continued eating in silence. She had finished her pasta and was about to take a sip of oolong tea when Erika said, "Norie, I really am jealous of you. If you and Okabe were dating you wouldn't be worrying about this kind of stuff. You're so confident. I bet you could convince Okabe's parents to see your way of thinking, no matter what." Erika's voice was mumbling, shaking, her gaze fixed down.

She closed her eyes, oolong tea still in

hand, as she thought on Erika's words. If she'd understood the Japanese correctly, not only was Erika jealous, but her remark was somewhat sardonic. She turned over Erika's words again and again in her head, scrutinizing each syllable for a few seconds to make sure she hadn't misunderstood.

She hadn't expected this development. Erika held a fundamental misunderstanding about her with no way of knowing how wrong it was; to Erika she was just another "normal" woman, same as her. Would coming out as a lesbian to Erika ease Erika's worries somewhat? Even if it did, she would then have to deal with the fallout of it spreading around the office. As she was running through these simulations in her head, she felt a twinge of anger. *Why should I have to feel this burden when it's everyone else who doesn't understand me?* More seconds went by as this flurry of thoughts descended on her.

"I should be getting back to work," Erika said, unable to stand the silence between them any longer.

"Wait," she said, as Erika stood up. She needed to at least say something. Erika stared at her. Even if she wasn't going to come out to her, she felt she had to say something to make her feel better.

"Good luck during Golden Week," was all she managed.

Erika left without another word.

It must have taken Erika a lot of courage to bare what she'd said just now. After all, Erika had been so desperate to carry out the pointless act of being jealous of her. It was so ridiculous a concept that she almost let out a laugh right there. A sadness immediately welled up inside her and the laugh turned into a sob in her throat.

In the end she neither laughed nor cried and went back to work alone.

It wasn't as if she didn't understand how Erika felt. The fear of loss, of being rejected, these were emotions she knew all too well. Every time she felt affection for someone, along with it came a deeply rooted fear, and should that affection be reciprocated, the fear only grew. And if she ever tried to be proactive, to pool her courage and overcome that fear, then she only ended up being beaten down by rejection and loss. She put on a brave face in front of everyone else, but she too felt pain, she too feared getting hurt. To keep herself safe from pain, she needed to continue to watch her step. She would have to keep on dancing alone in that complete and utter dark.

*Stop it.* She couldn't allow herself to fall into this hopeless way of thinking again. She put her mind back to her work. March was the busiest time of year and she needed to get through the bulk of it if she wanted to survive April.

"You not heading home yet, Chō?"

She returned to reality upon hearing Okabe's voice. Nine o'clock had come around before she realized, and it was just the two of them from their department left working. Outside, the city was cloaked in night sky, with the artificial lights from nearby office buildings providing the only source of life. Okabe had finished for the day and was getting ready to leave.

"I will shortly," she said.

"I thought *I* was a workaholic, but you've got me beat."

"You know us Capricorns," she said with a grin, suppressing the urge to ask about Erika.

Okabe laughed too. "All right, see you tomorrow," he said before he left.

She began to wrap up her work and left the office before too long.

It was past ten thirty by the time she got home. The empty apartment could be somewhat isolating, but this was one of the few places she could achieve the complete peace that comes from being completely alone. As she opened her front door to enter, the darkness inside seemed to spew out like mist. She threw herself onto her rug without turning on any of the lights and enjoyed the sensation of lying there for a moment.

The world is full of contradictions. And she was no exception. There was peace in the darkness, but within it lurked nightmares, too.

## CHAPTER 8

If only there had been a single ray of hope that night—this was the thing that plagued her every time she thought back to it.

She had achieved a good mark on her entrance exams in the February of her third year in high school and had passed her interview for the Japanese Literature course at National Taiwan University. Xiaoxue's grades on the other hand were less than ideal, and so she had decided to take the resits in July, a month after they were due to graduate from high school. Even as the blossoms of the royal poinciana burst into flame signalling the start of summer, Xiaoxue continued to focus on her studies with an almost manic obsession. It was hard to watch.

"I'm doing this for us—so we can enter the Rhododendron Palace together. So keep cheering me on, okay?" Xiaoxue said with a smile.

National Taiwan University—known to its students as Taida—was called the Rhododendron Palace due its fabulous bloom of rhododendron every spring.

"Of course. And when we get there we can ride our bikes down Royal Palm Boulevard when it's sunny, and when it's rainy we'll hole ourselves up in the Main Library. On clear nights, we'll watch the moon down by Drunken Moon Lake, and when it's overcast, we'll wander down Wenzhou Street and drink in its atmosphere instead."

She couldn't remember clearly anymore, but she was sure that was what she'd replied that day as the cacophonous waves of cicada cries had swept over them both. Xiaoxue laughed; her voice was as pure as those cicadas, before it flitted away into the sky as if borne on the damp spring breeze.

She waited at the entrance of the exam hall on the last day of Xiaoxue's Advanced Subjects Tests. The exam room may have been air-conditioned, but the heat outside was oppressive. Though there was no room in the cloudy midsummer sky for the blazing sun, those low storm clouds overhead rendered the day muggier than any clear day. She longed for the rains to come and clear the air.

The final exam of the day finished in the evening. Xiaoxue threaded through the rush of students, waving as she approached. The outcome of this exam would decide whether she and Xiaoxue would spend the next four years together or far apart. She was filled with a helplessness at this prospect. Beside her, Xiaoxue, finally finished with her exams, let out a grin as if a great weight had been lifted from her shoulders.

Feng Chia Night Market was over an hour by bus from their school, which meant they hardly ever went, but lured by the idea of eating street food and walking around the market stalls, they decided to go. The rush-hour bus was so crammed the two of them could barely move an inch, but holding Xiaoxue's hand gave her some comfort. By the time they got to the market it was already growing late, and the scattered neon displays gave off a distasteful glow. They weaved through the crowds, hand in hand, as they chewed on the market's fast food. They took the chance to try a variety of dishes: *jipai*, huge pieces of deep-fried chicken almost as large as their faces; *dachang bao xiaochang*, sausage meat wrapped in a glutinous rice bun. Grains of rice on their cheeks, oil smearing their lips —they couldn't help but laugh. *Even in summer, January plum blossoms and snow can still be connected*, she thought, stupidly.

As they walked down Wenhua Road, the market's main street, they passed by Feng Chia University. The campus stood there covered in darkness, oblivious to the shouts and foot traffic of the bustling night market. Tired from being on their feet for so long, they entered the campus as if it were the most natural next stop. The university was on summer holiday, too, and there were few people around. Before long, they encountered a fourteen-floor building with a small lawn before it, bordered by *gajumaru* trees. The two of them sat on a bench underneath one of the trees, the leaves hiding them from the glow of the lampposts nearby as the excitement of the market slowly dissipated from their hearts.

"It finally feels real. Our high school life is now over," Xiaoxue said, her gaze fixed on the night sky. The clouds were as heavy as ever.

"You do realize some of us graduated a month ago, don't you?"

"Hey, Yingmei, do you still want to die?" Xiaoxue asked suddenly.

"Well, I've never thought that I actually *want* to die, at least since meeting you. It's more that I have this feeling in my chest that I probably won't live long, if that makes sense."

"Why is that, do you think?"

Why indeed. She had no answer. She didn't doubt it had something to do with Danchen. And if that was the case, then did it also have something to do with the fact she was a lesbian? Although society had moved on since the nineties, the gay community continued to be ostracized from its expected pathways. Perhaps it was exactly because she was unable to grow up like a "normal person," get married, have kids, et cetera, that she couldn't visualize her own future, and she ended up fostering these attitudes towards death. But her life was now different to how it had been back in elementary school. The past year and a half that she had spent with Xiaoxue had allowed her to accept her sexuality as a part of herself. To understand that being gay wasn't a disease. To find out that Asia's largest pride parade was held every year in Taipei, the same parade she and Xiaoxue had agreed to attend once they started university. And so, if she was still worried about being a lesbian on some level, it seemed like such a betrayal to Xiaoxue.

Noting her silence, Xiaoxue went on, "Yingmei, you've lost someone special to you, haven't you?"

She wasn't expecting that remark. After all, she hadn't once mentioned Danchen— not on purpose, of course, she'd simply never felt any need to talk about what happened during her elementary school years. But it was no surprise that Xiaoxue of all people should have picked up on this, the same Xiaoxue who read everything she wrote so closely. She loved that side to Xiaoxue, but at times it made her feel stripped naked, as if Xiaoxue could see into every recess of her soul.

"Don't worry, as long as you're around I won't go off dying, okay?" she said, to change the topic, trying to hide her surprise.

"But what if I'm not around?"

"What do you mean? Are you going somewhere?"

"No, but ..." Xiaoxue sighed. "But you need to know that it's not a guarantee I'll always be by your side, Yingmei. I love you. So, please, promise me that you'll keep on living even if I'm not around anymore."

She felt a prickling sensation at being asked this so pointedly.

"I can't promise that. I don't want you to go. Besides, if you were to go, you'd be in no position to ask anything of me, let alone that."

"Yes, you're right ... I have no right to demand you to live your life in any particular way. But, still," Xiaoxue was silent for a moment before turning to look at her. Xiaoxue's eyes were full of tears. "Listen, Yingmei. I don't think I'll be able to get in to Taida."

So that was it. Xiaoxue had put on a cheerful front, but the exams were clearly bothering her.

"I screwed up the exams today," Xiaoxue went on. "I knew the answers, honestly I did, but when it came to actually picking the right one I began to doubt myself. Then during the next paper I realized where I'd chosen the wrong answers and started to panic. But then I'd overthink it again, and choose the wrong answer again."

Xiaoxue's emotions came welling forth and she started to sob. She wasn't sure what to do upon seeing Xiaoxue cry. All she could manage was to reach out a quivering hand and stroke her back. She really wanted to hug Xiaoxue tight enough that she would become a part of her, but she was scared of doing anything that might set her off.

"Nothing's set in stone yet, right? Who knows, maybe it went better than you thought? Let's just hope for the best, okay?"

Her inability to say anything better frustrated her—why, of all the thousands of words her eighteen years of life had given her, could she only come up with such a hackneyed string of phrases?

"Sorry, but I can't. It went badly, and I know because I was the one taking that test.

A miracle won't happen."

Xiaoxue leant in close to her and slumped her head onto her shoulder. The air felt more oppressive than earlier, the clouds so low it felt like they could come crashing down upon them at any moment. Still not a drop of rain had fallen from the sky. Crystal tears began to fall from Xiaoxue's cheek.

"I don't want to be away from you, Ying-mei, but ..."

She wasn't enough of a dreamer to believe that miracles existed either. Despite that, she wished for one now.

"We won't be apart, not really. Even if you don't get into Taida, there's a bunch of other good universities in Taipei. What about Chengchi University? They've got a ton of literature and foreign-language courses. A lot of famous writers and artists graduated from there, too."

Even as she was saying these words, she felt despair in her heart. It didn't matter how good the courses at Chengchi were. It wasn't part of the future they had drawn up together—spring days admiring the rhododendrons, autumn afternoons reciting poetry to each other. There were so many classes they wished to take together, so many bookstores they wanted to peruse. These daydreams had been weaved together day after day, made more concrete as they researched the syllabus, the independent bookshops near the university. What Xiaoxue was upset at was that their dream had been destroyed by her own hand. What could she say to her in this situation?

But before she could offer any further words of support, Xiaoxue spoke.

"I'm going to take a year out."

This announcement shocked her. Surely she didn't have to go so far as to delay her university life by a whole year?

Xiaoxue kept on speaking, as if talking to herself, head still resting on her shoulder.

"I made a promise to my parents that if I didn't get into Taida I would take a year out and try again. They're both Taida alumni and always go on about how they want me to get in. Listen, Yingmei, I've already made up my mind. I'll meet their expectations, and in return I'll convince them to accept us."

Her heart twinged with pain. This was the

first she had heard of this. Xiaoxue was always so calm and collected, always seemed to be treading a path she had chosen for herself. It was a shock to hear that this was how she wanted her parents to accept her sexuality. This wasn't merely a simple desire; she had worked out a whole plan to achieve it.

She couldn't do something like that. She was so scared of the uncertainty of the future that she imagined one day she would choose death as a way to escape facing it head on. But, unlike her, drawn so strongly to a liberating death that she ignored the future before her, here was Xiaoxue thinking not only of her own future but also of their shared one. She needed to support Xiaoxue. She needed to show that she was on her side. She needed to, but still, but still …

"Don't go, Xiaoxue."

She knew she was being selfish. She had no right to affect the decisions that Xiaoxue had made for herself, and she hated herself for being this way. But she couldn't not say anything. Xiaoxue's house was in Taichung, which meant that she would attend a cram school there. On the other hand she would be moving to Taipei. Although the two cities were only two hundred kilometres apart, this distance felt vaster to her than the distance between heaven and earth.

"I don't want to, Yingmei," Xiaoxue said quietly. "But this isn't only about my parents. I want to enter the Rhododendron Palace too. And I want to live my university life with you. So, please, I know I'm being selfish but wait for me, just for one year. I'll be with you before you know it, and then we can follow Qiu Miaojin ourselves, to Drunken Moon Lake, down Tingzhou Road, Wenzhou Street … We'll rewrite *Notes of a Crocodile* so that it doesn't end in tragedy."

Her mind drifted to that day, over a year in the future, where they would meet again, strolling down the pier by Drunken Moon Lake in the night breeze, seeking out the hidden bookshops on Tingzhou Road … Xiaoxue hadn't said anything the slightest bit selfish. All she was doing was taking the required steps to achieve her dream. So why did she rebuke her for that?

"It's like Du Fu said, 'Our lives do not meet, like two stars in the night,'" she moaned, like a small child wanting to be appeased.

"Don't say things like that. It's not as if we're going to be apart for twenty years or anything. After all, didn't Wang Bo say, 'It is a fact of life that our paths diverge, but I shall dampen my handkerchief with you, my dear.'"

"But that's referring to a little girl. It's not as if she could do anything about it anyway."

Xiaoxue lifted her head up and briefly embraced her before stroking her hair. The two of them fell silent again. The only sounds were the bustle of the distant Feng Chia Night Market. The sky was a featureless dark.

They parted ways at the bus stop, heading home on different buses. The twelve-thirty bus back from the night market was crowded, but her heart still retained a warmth as she was bustled by the rocking bus and the crowd for the hour-long trip, holding on to a handle. She could still feel Xiaoxue's heat, her perfume still wafted around her. She would be fine; they would be fine. It wasn't as if their relationship was solely romantic in nature; their bond would not break over the measly course of a year.

Disembarking the bus and walking home, this was the only thought in her mind. Taichung and Taipei weren't so far as to prevent them from meeting up during the year either. Xiaoxue had supported her so much during their high school years, so now it was time for her to return the favour. As she came to this realization, her body felt lighter. Yes, even if they couldn't meet in person, they could always phone each other to give support. Xiaoxue was clever and dependable; next year's exams would go just fine. There was nothing to worry about—

She felt a jolt from behind. Before she could register what was happening, she was thrust onto the ground—arms were grabbing her arm and neck, a cloth or rag was stuffed into her mouth, her body pinned down. There were no streetlights around, and the sky above, filled with roiling clouds, was devoid of light. She looked around and saw she was in a small, deserted alleyway. She came through this way every day on the way home, but she had never, until now, realized how dark it was. She heard laboured breathing by her ear. It was coming from the person pushing her down. Her arms and legs were forced down; she couldn't budge an inch. Twisting her head, she saw a man she didn't recognize. His balding head and face were covered in sweat. She pooled her strength and tried to force him off, but her body wouldn't move; she tried to scream, but no sound came out. The man spread his body, keeping her limbs pinned down as he began to grope her all over. The image of Xiaoxue wandered into her mind's eye. Thinking of that beautiful face sent a wave of pain through her heart that was dozens if not hundreds times worse than the one her body felt. Her vision began to blur with tears and the foul man above her started to fade from view. *I told you, Xiaoxue. I told you I probably wouldn't live long.* The man's horrid breath carried with it the smell of decay, like that of rotting fish. She felt the bile rise in her throat. *The thorn bird? The most beautiful song in the world? Life isn't like that. I'm going to die here and now. It will be meaningless, it'll just be disgusting, and ugly, and—*

When she came to the man was gone. In his place a small crowd of concerned onlookers were gathered around her. Someone was talking on the phone. Her body hurt all over. The sky above was still devoured by the dark. In the distance she heard police sirens. The smell of mould and dead fish continued to hang in the air. Tears welled from her eyes before trickling onto the grimy asphalt. Although the man was gone, the last words he had spoken before she blacked out echoed in her head.

"Don't like men, eh, you fucking dyke? Well, I'll show you a good time ..."

## CHAPTER 9

If she weren't a lesbian, would she have avoided such a fate? She knew that ifs and maybes didn't exist in the real world, but she couldn't help wondering: *Is the stigmatization of my sexuality the source of all my misfortune?* This illogical question had plagued her for a long time.

She was still unsure whether she could say she was proud of her sexuality, but she chose to head to Tokyo's Rainbow Pride festival. It fell during the week-long string of national holidays in early May known as Golden Week —however, for Japan's LGBT community, it's less golden and more rainbow coloured. Although she had never been to Taipei's own pride parade, this was her third time at Tokyo Pride, held as always in Yoyogi Park.

The last national holiday of that year's

Golden Week fell on a Sunday. By the time she arrived at 11 a.m., the event space of Yoyogi Park was already crammed with attendees. Having spent long enough in Tokyo's lesbian spaces, it was obvious how small the community was. At every event she was almost guaranteed to bump into several acquaintances or friends. It wasn't rare for someone she had met years ago to be dating someone she had become friends with only months since. Today was no different, and she had barely taken her first steps into the festival area before seeing and greeting a number of people she knew.

The festival was made up of a variety of groups—from those running food or drink stalls and jewellery pop-ups to those performing on the main stage—and everything was plastered in rainbow stripes, the symbol of diversity. While here, she almost fell into the blissful assumption that the world was devoid of hate and discord, but this never lasted. No matter how many times she read the heartwarming slogans, *Love and Peace* or *It Gets Better*, they simply rang hollow to her.

She met with Sho, Sophia, and two other lesbian friends from Taiwan by the main stage. Most Taiwanese lesbians in Tokyo knew each other, thanks to an online community founded by Sho shortly after arriving in the city.

Soon enough Aki arrived. Aki and Sho were like two peas in a pod, and since meeting through a lesbian dating app, although simply friends at first, they had begun to attend club nights together before finally announcing that they were a couple. While Sho had an androgynous short haircut, thick-framed black glasses, and rather boyish, edgy clothes, Aki was her complete opposite, with long brown curly hair and a feminine wardrobe. Although their looks couldn't have been more different, they shared a laid-back personality and an uncaring attitude to what people thought about them. They flirted wherever and whenever without a care for anyone who might be watching. Sophia had taken a snap of them making out at the club night back in February and since going viral in the community they had become minor celebrities. In the wake of this, instead of worrying about what others might think, their open love for one another became more blatant.

Befitting its name, the weather at the end of Golden Week was perfect, with the sun casting golden halos in the air. They left the festival area and registered to join the actual parade, and then joined the crowd to get ready for the parade's journey around Shibuya.

"Did you get round to reading that Kaho Nakayama book I recommended?" she asked Sophia, filling in the dead space before the parade set off. Two years older than her, Sophia had studied Chinese Literature at university and was a booklover too. Alongside her office job in Tokyo, she helped a few friends in Miaoli, Taiwan, to run an independent bookshop called Langyuan. Living far away meant that her work was mostly things that could be done remotely, such as organizing events and liaising with authors, but she occasionally took paid leave to help out with any in-store events. As a result, Sophia's life was rather hectic, and she'd only returned from Taiwan yesterday so that she could come today.

"Yeah. I got a paperback of *To the Abyss of the White Rose*," Sophia said.

"What did you think?"

"You know, from the flowing prose, the aura of predestined tragedy, and the depiction of a full-on, self-destructive love that has no room for any logical reason, I could see a lot of similarities to Qiu Miaojin's writing. You know, Xiaohui, I see what you meant when you said that if Qiu Miaojin hadn't died, she would have written a book like this." Sophia was a fellow fan of Qiu and had just started up a Qiu Miaojin book club at her bookshop. "But I don't think she would ever have written about having no interest in feminism or gay pride parades. Qiu was aware of the fact that even if one creates some kind of spiritual utopia in one's novels, it is impossible to separate one's personal worries from politics. If she'd been alive in 2003 when the first pride parade took place in Taiwan, I think she would have been out there on the front lines, waving the flag for the LGBT community."

Sophia often attended demonstrations and had helped to lead the charge during the

Sunflower Student Movement in 2014. The Sunflower protestors had occupied the Legislative Yuan, and she was one of the first to enter. There, Sophia had provided Japanese-Chinese interpretation as well as streaming the situation inside the building to Japanese audiences. Some of her coworkers at Langyuan were also involved in the movement, and they made their bookshop a small base for leftist activism.

"Even so, don't you think the whole parade would have exacerbated Qiu's inner nonconformist nature?" she said.

Sophia paused before replying: "You're not completely wrong there, but, well, I don't think there's that same kind of nonconformity in Nakayama's works. You know, living through a tumultuous time, it—"

"Nakayama? Shō Nakayama, as in Sun Yat-sen? I know he was a bit of a womanizer, but that's kind of a weird topic of conversation, don't you think?" Sho chimed in. Unable to understand their Chinese, Aki simply looked on blankly.

"*Kaho* Nakayama—the Japanese author, not the Chinese politician. For someone whose name has the meaning of 'reading' in it, you really don't read much at all, do you?" Sophia said with an exasperated look. She couldn't help but burst into laughter at the ridiculousness of their serious literary discussion being sidetracked into gossip about Sun Yat-sen's sex life. Soon enough the parade set off.

The parade departs from the Shibuya City Office and makes its way over the famous scramble crossing by Shibuya Station before returning to Yoyogi Park via Omotesandō. The participants of the parade held placards with their own personal slogans emblazoned upon them, waved rainbow flags, and high-fived the cheering passersby as the crowd made its journey. Sophia had her own placard written in multiple colours: *We don't need red papers; give us a blue bird instead.* She thought Sophia's scathing criticism of the government's recent military legislation fused with a reference to Chinese mythology carried quite a clever message.

The float that led the parade blared out club music, and aboard it a number of flamboyantly dressed drag queens danced above the crowds. Their energy was infectious, and soon enough the whole parade was clapping their hands in time with the beat and moving their bodies as the parade progressed. Surrounded by the vibrant festival, her heart felt somewhat lighter. On a glorious day like today, under the bountiful sunlight and surrounded by a rainbow of colour, she almost felt as if she could push the darkness within her a little bit away. The fragments of memory that circled her mind were filtered down into simple images, unable to exacerbate her pain and simply laying on the surface of awareness. It felt as though the dark mists permanently plaguing a dangerous mountain path had finally lifted. Even if only temporarily, she could breathe. These moments of reprieve had happened a few times since coming to Japan, but this was the first time since her twenty-seventh birthday.

Out of nowhere, Erika's smiling face and bell-like laughter appeared in her mind. The day after that lunch on that Monday in February, Erika had appeared at her desk first thing to apologize for storming off in silence. She was happy they had made up, but she noticed that she felt a sadness too. During that lunch Erika had seemed at a complete loss, had said how jealous of her she was— this kind of emotional response was human, or so she thought. But before even twenty-four hours had passed, Erika had faced her own weakness, had decided to overcome her doubts and jealousy. As she watched Erika apologize, she wondered if she could ever be that honest with herself.

The night before Pride, she and Erika met for dinner. Erika had just come back from Nagano and wanted to tell her about the meeting with Okabe's parents. It turned out Erika's worries had been completely unfounded, and thanks to Okabe's help, she had completely won over his parents. Afraid that their son, who all throughout school had focused only on studying, would never find a girlfriend, they were apparently relieved to find that he had met such a lovely woman. Erika's smile as she related her time in Nagano was the picture of happiness. Despite the loneliness gnawing at her heart, she was happy at Erika's good fortune. But when Erika asked, "So what kind of guys are you into, Norie?" all she could do was avoid the question as far as possible.

The parade soon reached the crossroads at Jinnan Itchōme, where the nearby Marui department store was emblazoned with a rainbow flag. This was exactly why she liked Pride. It was one of the few places outside of that quiet darkness of her apartment where her heart could relax. Under the streaks of cirrus clouds across the cobalt sky, this proud rainbow-coloured group marched forward. It felt as if the world were celebrating. Of course, she knew this was nothing more than an illusion hiding the world's discord, but she relied on it.

Upon reaching Shibuya's crossing, the group turned left under the gaze of thousands of spectators. She glanced over at Sophia walking next to her. Sophia was far more pragmatic than she was, and she could imagine Sophia leaning over to say something like, "This group tied together by something so superficial, this carnival-like parade—it has no real meaning as a social movement." Sophia's viewpoint might be true, but she couldn't accept that. She needed to shield her eyes from the feeling that this crowd, although unified on the surface, was full of unconnected strangers. She needed to force herself to find something for her heart to rely upon. If not, then her everyday life would collapse from beneath her.

It was as the parade passed under the railway bridge that she saw Kaori. Immediately she started to shake. She turned away as quickly as she could, trying not to meet Kaori's gaze, but her body was already covered in a cold sweat. She could feel her pulse beginning to race, her heart beginning to palpitate. She had only seen Kaori for a second—standing on the road next to the parade, gleaming as she held up her *Equality for all love* placard and high-fived the marchers—but the image had burned itself into her mind. Upon seeing her pale face, Sophia asked, "Are you okay?"

"It's nothing," she replied immediately, trying her best to put on a normal expression. Sophia didn't probe any further. The parade moved onward as if nothing had happened, and the place where Kaori had stood passed into the distance behind them. She wasn't sure if Kaori had seen her, but that moment taught her that her fear was as strong as ever.

## CHAPTER 10

On that dark night, due to the genitals and semen of a man whose face she couldn't remember, her life was split in two. Until that moment, thanks to writing she had been able to overcome the feeling of loss that lurked in her heart, and thanks to Xiaoxue she was able to even seize some form of happiness, but ever since, she had been stuck free-falling into a bottomless abyss. Love, fiction, all those things she once viewed as beautiful were unreachable from this abyss —all that existed around her was a cold, unending dark. Not even Xiaoxue could save her from this pit.

She didn't know whether that man was ever caught, nor did she care. It wasn't as if his arrest would erase this disaster.

Her memories were like a shredded roll of

film scattered around her. First there were the sounds. Voices she recognized and those she did not fluttered into her ears. "Why was she walking down that alleyway all alone at night?" "She's only eighteen, the poor thing." "I ought to warn my own daughter to be careful, too." Next was her sense of touch. She felt a horrible lurching feeling, as if she were being carried. Then came smell. A concoction of alcoholic disinfectant and medicines—the smell of a hospital. After that, sight. The first thing that filtered into her eyes after she finally managed to open them was the clinical light of a hospital. Then, pain. Her whole body was in pain. In particular, the space between her legs felt as if she had been scorched with a white-hot piece of iron. Then sight, again. Two silhouettes that appeared to be her parents floated vaguely at the periphery of her field of view. A figure that appeared to be a doctor came into view, asked a question; she replied. Suddenly everything before her went dark. A deep, dreamless sleep.

She didn't know how many times she repeated this cycle of waking in the clinical hospital ward and falling back into a dead sleep. Her memories only became a solid mass again after she returned to her parents' home. She was back in that same old third-floor room, surrounded by her familiar things. Outside the window, the expanse of fields stretched out into the distance as it had done before. Everything was so familiar, but nothing felt real, almost as if she were separated from it by a vast emptiness. This was a similar-looking but completely different world. She had already realized she would never be able to go back to the world she had once lived in.

Her door opened and she heard someone come in. She flinched as her eyes snapped to the doorway.

It was her mother. Of course it was, she knew that. Yet for some reason the person standing at the door seemed like a complete stranger from a distant planet. Or, to be more accurate, it didn't seem like a person at all, but rather a doll or mannequin or something that had simply taken on a human form.

"Were you already up?" her mother asked. In her hands was a bowl of noodles. *Right. It's lunchtime already*, she thought, almost as if she were thinking of someone else's schedule.

"Yeah," she said with a quick nod.

"You must be hungry. Here, Yingmei, I made your favourite: beef noodle soup. It's hot, so you don't have to rush eating it, okay?" Her mother placed the bowl on her desk. Above the desk was a photo, that photo from fourth grade of her classmates sitting around the school organ. *Danchen, that was her name. Of course, I forgot that had happened,* she thought, staring at the photograph.

"Don't dwell on this more than you have to, okay? Soon you'll be off to university and you'll be having fun all the time," her mother said. Staring at her silent daughter, her mother reached out her arms in an embrace. Immediately, she recoiled. Her mother dropped her arms with a sigh.

"Rest up once you've eaten. I'll come get the bowl later," she said before quietly leaving the room.

She stared over at her lunch. Steam floated from the surface of the soup. She moved herself to her desk and picked up her chopsticks, but she wasn't hungry in the slightest. All of a sudden, her phone started buzzing. The name on the screen was Xiaoxue's.

A deep fear started to well up in her, and her body began to tremble. *I've been punished because Xiaoxue and I did something wrong.* She felt that this was true. It must be. If she hadn't fallen in love with Xiaoxue; if she weren't a lesbian—at the same time as these thoughts, a small voice in her head began to whisper: *Being gay isn't a disease, it isn't a crime. You've done nothing wrong. It's all his fault.* She knew this was the voice of reason. But, no, if she hadn't been with Xiaoxue, if they hadn't been out so late—no, this is the twenty-first century, it's outdated to think that a woman walking alone at night is to blame—true as that may be the fact remains that you met him and your life has been turned upside down; and that's the truth no matter how much you harp on about stupid things like equality or human rights—

"Hello? Yingmei?"

She tapped the answer button with a shaking finger and Xiaoxue's voice came out of the speaker. She needed to say something.

Something so that Xiaoxue wouldn't worry. But what?

"Hello? I heard you'd been discharged from hospital. Are you at your parents' now? I went to the hospital a bunch of times, but they said they weren't allowing friends to visit, and, well, I couldn't say we were dating, so ..."

The usual traces of calm in Xiaoxue's voice were gone and she was speaking quickly, as if under some kind of pressure. Xiaoxue seemed unsure of what best to do, as if she were on the verge of tears. *See? Even she won't tell anyone about your relationship ...*

The powerless rational part of her brain could do nothing in the face of this growing, black fear. She hung up on Xiaoxue and returned the room to its silence.

Two months later, she left her parents' home as scheduled and flung herself into the bustling city of Taipei. As predicted, Xiaoxue's grades weren't good enough to get into Taida, so she decided to take a year out to try again.

Taipei was different from how she had imagined, covered by a clouded sky all year long. Spring brought muggy rains, summer was visited by whipping, wild storms and typhoons, and winter signalled the monsoon season. Most of the year it rained, and the Rhododendron Palace was no exception to this foul weather.

She didn't join any university clubs and simply attended her lectures while refusing to engage with anyone. Even in her Japanese-language classes where the students were required to pair up for conversational practice, she was always alone, as if this were the most natural thing in the world. As soon as lectures were over, she would return to her dorm room and lose herself in Murakami and Dazai. When hungry, she would head to the canteen and buy the minimum amount before returning to her room to eat it. At 10 p.m., Xiaoxue's classes would end and they would talk on the phone.

"They probably think I'm dirty," she said one day, her voice full of self-derision.

Xiaoxue was the only person she spoke with and the only outlet for her feelings, which meant that Xiaoxue was the target of all the roiling emotions in her chest.

"Of course they don't. And you're not dirty—I love you, after all."

"How can you of all people say that? I'm dirty, through and through. Our relationship isn't right. It'll just lead to destruction."

"Nothing's going to be destroyed. There's nothing wrong with our relationship. You need to be more confident, Yingmei."

"Tell that to the world, not me. Tell it to your parents—that we're going out."

"I ... will. One day, I promise."

"Why 'one day'? Why not now? You think they won't accept us unless you get into a good university."

Their phone conversations would always escalate into a one-sided verbal assault. Each day she would spend every hour from morning through to evening looking forward to speaking to Xiaoxue, but when they finally did speak, she would always make Xiaoxue cry. For some reason, she could never say what she wanted and instead ended up forcing her darkest emotions on Xiaoxue. Xiaoxue's everyday life was filled with nothing but study, and instead of supporting her, she only succeeded in worsening the burden on Xiaoxue's shoulders. When she heard Xiaoxue's exhausted voice and imagined how tired she must look, she was assaulted by a wave of guilt and self-disgust. Despite it all, Xiaoxue never lost her temper and always did her best to appease her. No matter how pitifully she acted, Xiaoxue always tried to pull her out of her despair.

"Yingmei, we dreamed about one day entering the Rhododendron Palace, and now you're finally there. Don't focus on the bad stuff, how about trying to enjoy things a bit more?"

"Enjoy things? In the midwinter? It's cold and it rains every day. I'm sick of it."

"Well, why don't you join a club and meet some new people? Taida has a lesbian society, doesn't it?"

"I get it. You're sick of me, too. You're just dying to push me onto other people, aren't you?"

"No, I'm not. All I want is for you to enjoy your time and—"

"I'm not joining any club. They'll end up grouping together when I'm not there and talking behind my back. I know they will."

Her solitary nature made a lot of the fellow students on her course uncomfortable around her. Unlike most of her classmates, she had been studying Japanese since junior high school and had already progressed to reading a lot of Japanese literature in the original, making her top of the class. This only served to worsen her solitude. Taichung Girls' Senior High School was prestigious, and so a lot of its students went on to study at National Taiwan University, which meant that news of the assault a few months ago had spread among the students in her degree course.

"Why does she have to put on that face that screams 'I'm the most unfortunate person in the entire world'?"

"If she just acted normally, we wouldn't care."

"Maybe she likes being the tragic heroine?"

Whenever she walked around the university, she couldn't help feeling that those around her were talking behind her back, and this paranoia was often justified when she caught scraps of conversation. She wasn't sure anymore who she could and could not trust. As the Chinese saying goes: *In the forest, the trees look like soldiers; the sound of the wind and the birds are frightening.* In her mind, anyone could be an enemy.

Once, a slight, friendly-looking girl in her year came up to her and said, "I'm sure you went through a lot, Yingmei. But do your best, I'm on your side, okay?"

She didn't know how to respond and was silent for a moment. However, as the girl made no move to leave, as if awaiting a response, she said simply: "Sorry, I'd rather you not bring it up."

The girl's face changed in an instant, and she left without another word. The next time she bumped into this girl, she had already joined the ranks of those who spoke ill of her. When walking past, the girl said in a deliberately loud voice, "I took the time to talk to her, but she wasn't in the least bit grateful. What kind of weirdo behaves like that?" Her fear of people grew yet deeper, and she fled the spot, flinging herself under the covers as soon as she got back to her dorm—her body shaking uncontrollably.

Each university dorm room was occupied by four people: a twenty-square-metre space containing four loft beds with desks underneath. So as not to disturb her three roommates, she took her calls with Xiaoxue in the corridor, but she would often lose herself and end up shouting angrily. Whenever she came back into the room, her roommates looked at her with disdain, and eventually she was given a warning by the dorm manager. Soon enough, even the dorms became too difficult a space for her to be in, so from her second semester she began renting a private place outside the university. When she relayed this development, Xiaoxue fell silent before saying with some difficulty, "Yingmei, I think you should maybe see a doctor or someone."

She was shocked to hear this.

"What do you mean by that? Are you saying I'm sick or something?"

"Well, we won't know until you go, will we?"

"No, go on. What am I sick with, huh?"

"I just said I didn't know if you *were* sick!" Xiaoxue said, her voice raised. She flinched upon hearing this uncharacteristic outburst from Xiaoxue.

Of course, she was aware that her behaviour was not normal. But acknowledging it was too scary, so she had refused to face the fact. But now that Xiaoxue had vocalized the matter, she had to face up to it whether she liked it or not.

Xiaoxue went on in a quiet voice coated in a faint hopelessness.

"I'm sorry, Yingmei. I can't go on like this, I'll end up crazy too. I tried my best, I decided to be strong for you, to help heal your wounds, to support you. But I guess I wasn't strong enough. If we go on like this, it won't just be getting into Taida that'll be hard, my whole life will fall to pieces."

She suppressed the urge to cry and scream as she waited for Xiaoxue to finish.

The logical part of her understood—Xiaoxue was only human, and not only that, she was struggling with taking a year out after high school. She couldn't expect Xiaoxue to deal with the tumultuous waves of her emotions, nor did Xiaoxue have any obligation to do so. To Xiaoxue, she was a deep abyss in which any light she shone, however warm, was engulfed by the bottomless dark.

Xiaoxue had already done so much to help. She didn't want to lose her. She should apologize, promise that she'd go to a hospital, expend the tiniest amount of effort to lessen Xiaoxue's load, tell Xiaoxue that she was the most important thing in her life. The logical part of her knew this. But, still—

"Is that how it is? You finally want to break up, do you? I told you, didn't I, that everything would be destroyed? It's because we were together that I went through what I did. But still you—"

—*want to get rid of me*, was what she couldn't say. Xiaoxue wasn't getting rid of her, no, she was the one who was pushing Xiaoxue away.

Xiaoxue had nothing to say to this tirade. The only words she said in a quiet, exhausted voice were, "Yingmei, I'm sorry," before the line went dead and an emotionless beeping rang emptily into her ear.

She hurled her phone at the wall. With an explosive crack it split into pieces and the room fell into silence once more. She felt dizzy. It felt as if the sky had turned in on itself. The blood in her body turned cold, as if she had been thrust into a casing of ice. Her heart ached so much that she wanted to grab a knife and cut it out. It was only when she put a box cutter to her wrists and stared at the blood trickling out that the pain began to abate. Drained of energy, she buried herself in her bed.

The next day she started seeing a doctor from the psychiatric department at the university's hospital.

## CHAPTER 11

Kaori Takada. The only other woman that she had truly loved, apart from Xiaoxue.

When they first met, she felt as if she'd come to the end of a long journey and had been blessed with a wonderful fortune from the heavens. She had gone so far as to cross the seas to escape her past, and those efforts had come to fruition—finally she had met someone who accepted all of her.

It was during the autumn of her twenty-sixth year that she met Kaori through a dating app. The three and a half years since she had come to Japan had passed in a blink of an eye, and before she knew it, she had started and completed her master's degree and had been working already for a year and a half. She had been free of any particular misfortunes and had enjoyed a normal yet peaceful everyday life. She was still on antidepressants, but the dosage was lower compared to her university days, and thanks to the pills her mental state was stable; she was able to live a life no different to anyone else's.

She wasn't the sort of person who wants to meet someone they've connected with online straight away, so she and Kaori spent a while messaging each other, until a month or so later when Kaori suggested they go to an art gallery together.

Ueno Station on a public holiday was filled with swathes of people in every direction, like swarms of locusts. She had arrived first and was standing next to a pillar outside the ticket gates reading a book when she felt a pair of eyes upon her. She looked up and saw a woman in her late twenties, her short black hair tinged with red, weaving through the crowd, walking towards her. She knew instantly that it was Kaori. Her easygoing, plain outfit of a grey jumper and high-waisted denim skirt suggested the free-spirited nature of an art-school student. Her height and looks were nothing special, you might even say her face was plain, the sort of woman you would see in a crowd then forget about not long after. But upon a second or third look, you would begin to notice a carefully honed allure to her appearance.

Feeling it would be somewhat embarrassing if Kaori spotted her first, she returned the book to her bag and gave a wave.

The art gallery was holding a special Van Gogh exhibition. She wasn't that clued up about art and didn't know even the famous stories about Van Gogh—that he had cut off his left ear and given it to the woman he loved, or that he had killed himself with a gun. Despite this, wandering the exhibition with Kaori was incredibly fun. Kaori had graduated from an art school and now lectured at one, and so was especially knowledgeable about Western art and told tales about each piece as they walked by. These assessments filled her in on the use of colour and its link to Van Gogh's mental state, about how he was influenced by the *ukiyo-e* movement, his relationships with his contemporaries—things she would never have known about if she'd come on her own. It was a different emotional world from the world of literature she had so far dipped her toes in.

More dates followed the first, and although neither of them openly proposed the idea of a relationship they both were silently aware that they had surpassed simple friendship.

Their second date was to a museum, their third to a modern literature institute. By the time they left the institute, the evening sun was already sinking to the west, and the late autumn sea breeze was cold to the skin. They entered a nearby café and began to talk art, literature, and politics as they always did.

"*Our hearts are connected, like that invisible thread* ... as they say," she said with a smile during a pause in their conversation, quoting Li Shangyin.

"What's that mean?" Kaori asked, oblivious to the reference, which was now a popular phrase in China.

"Oh, nothing," she said with a laugh, closing the topic.

As Han Yu said: *All fields bear experts.* An art graduate, Kaori had as much knowledge about Japanese literature as most other people, but naturally knew nothing of the

Chinese or Taiwanese canon. Once, Kaori drew together all her knowledge on the Chinese writings she had studied in middle school and came out with this observation on the poem "Spring View" by Du Fu:

*"Even upon the fall of a nation, the mountains and rivers remain / In the city, plants grow thick with the arrival of spring,"* Kaori recited. "When I think of this poem, I can always feel the breath of living creatures. A collapsed nation still welcomes the coming of spring and plants will begin to thrive again with the premonition of rebirth. Whenever I see those Syrian refugee camps on TV, it's just so painful; it makes me hope that their spring comes sooner."

She listened to Kaori while secretly smiling to herself—Kaori's reading was simply so far off the mark. Kaori didn't know how much of an effect the An Lushan Rebellion had had on the Tang dynasty. The most developed city in the world of the eighth century, Chang'an, was reduced to ashes in a single night. Afterwards, the Tang dynasty instead followed a path towards decline. *Plants grow thick* wasn't what Kaori described it as, a premonition of rebirth; it was an image used to illustrate a ruined city, devoid of people, covered now only in weeds. If Kaori had only remembered the next verse, *Feeling the passage of time, I shed tears even as I look at the flowers / I mourn parting, and seeing the birds, too, fills my heart with pain*, then she would have surely come to a different conclusion. Despite forgetting this key verse, the humanitarian aspect of Kaori's interpretation, linking this piece to the plight of Syrian refugees, wasn't unlike the timeless poet Du Fu. It was this part of Kaori that she found herself drawn to.

But the world they lived in wasn't spring; it was drawing into a deep winter. As the year came to a close, she invited Kaori to her home, where they met for the sixth time to enjoy New Year's Eve together. The evening was spent in the most ordinary way—eating snacks, watching the annual Kōhaku Song Contest on TV, and enjoying each other's company—but for some reason as she did these things with Kaori, the word *happiness* flitted through her mind over and over. As the chimes of the temple purification bell that ring in the New Year faded away, she leaned into Kaori and held her hand in hers. She gently stroked Kaori's hair with her other hand, and they enjoyed a moment of peace together.

"I've missed the last train," Kaori said quietly after a moment.

Kaori lived south of Tokyo in Yokohama, yet it seemed she didn't realize that New Year's Eve was the one time of year where the trains ran all night. This was surprising as she herself knew this despite only having lived in Tokyo for three and a half years. It wouldn't be hard for Kaori to return from Shinjuku to Yokohama, but she decided to keep this knowledge to herself.

"If they're not running, then why don't we board the dream express, and ride the galactic railroad into the stars, just the two of us."

"On an endless adventure."

"I wouldn't want it to end, so I wouldn't mind."

How long had it been since she'd said such sweet nothings? Separated by two thousand kilometres of sea, all that time before she came to Japan seemed like distant memories of a previous existence. It seemed that the dark shadow of those memories hadn't managed to chase her all the way here. Kaori seemed to shine a light, soft like moonlight, that managed to cast away the aura of death that swathed her heart.

"*When I think of you / I truly wish for this life / a once needless thing / to grant me just enough time / so that one day we may meet,*" she said quoting a poem by Fujiwara no Yoshitaka. "It's weird. When I'm with you, Kaori, I think that maybe I don't want to die quite yet."

"Oh yeah? I wouldn't mind dying now, to be honest."

"You wouldn't mind dying? Wait a second, are you using Futabatei Shimei's translation of 'I love you' to express your feelings for me?"

"Well, would you prefer me to phrase it using the line his dad said to him? I know Shimei's well respected now, but I remember reading that his dad hated his writing and famously told him to 'Just fuck off and die!'"

"Well, that's because Futabatei Shimei was a guy, I guess. But I wouldn't mind if you phrased it either way, Kaori. In fact, I'd be happy, really happy."

"If we die together, then maybe we'll be able to cross the Sanzu River together. We won't need some man pulling us across."

"Pulling us across? What are you talking about?"

"Didn't you know? It's a Japanese myth that says when a woman dies and has to cross the Sanzu River to the afterlife, she needs to be pulled across it by the man she lost her virginity to."

As Kaori said this, a flicker of unease passed through her mind. She chose to ignore it.

"What a stupid myth. There's a limit to how much misogyny and heteronormative bullshit a story can have."

"Well, old legends are mostly like that."

"Why the hell should I care about the Sanzu River or whatever? Death should be the end to everything—if not I couldn't take it. I don't need another life after this one, thanks."

"Then ... let's enjoy the time we have while still alive."

Saying this, Kaori drew her into the bed. She smiled at the fact Kaori was inviting her back to her own bed, but she drew close anyway. *She's right—I'm still alive.* It had been a long time since she had felt as alive as this.

The two of them lay on her single bed, face to face, as Kaori reached out with her pale hands, putting them under her clothes, and began to stroke her body all over—her stomach, her hips, her breasts, her back. Those slender fingers, so suited to holding a paintbrush, seemed to be coated in an electricity that sent tingles of pleasure wherever they touched. No matter what injury she might meet with, she was sure Kaori's hands would prove more healing than any medicine.

"Are you okay, Rie? You're shaking. Are you scared?"

"No, it's just static shock from the sparks between us. It feels like electricity running through my body."

"That's proof that our hearts are one."

Kaori's hands slipped inside her bra and began to stroke her nipples. Her breath caught in her throat as she wrapped her arms around Kaori.

"That's a tight hug," Kaori said.

"It's so I don't lose you."

"I'm not going anywhere. We're going to head beyond the stars together, aren't we?"

She smiled at Kaori's reply. She knew it was unrealistic, a meaningless joke, but she wanted nothing more than to wallow in those sweet words. Whatever rational root love might emerge from, it's a ridiculous emotion: the polar opposite of logic. If true meaning lies only in tragedy, then the world of someone completely and deeply in love is a comedy, full of nothing but pure farce. And in such a world, she was aware meaning was not meant to be sought; it's enough to simply enjoy it.

Kaori's hands began to pull off her clothes. She had been mentally preparing for this moment since she first decided Kaori could stay over; but now, with her top in the process of being removed, her body shuddered and she reflexively stopped Kaori.

"What's wrong?" Kaori asked, surprise tinging her voice. What could she say? She spent a few seconds considering what words would be best before giving up on the idea of explaining what she had felt.

"I can take it off myself."

She was able to take her own clothes off without much difficulty. Kaori hesitated for a moment before taking her clothes off too, then climbing over her she began to kiss her—her breasts, the nape of her neck, her earlobe. She felt a bit squashed by Kaori but chose to be enraptured by the silly thought that it was the weight of happiness pressing upon her.

Perhaps feeling that the glare of the ceiling light was ruining the mood somewhat, Kaori flicked off the lights. In the darkness she felt Kaori's lips meet hers. Kaori's tongue forced itself into her mouth and, wishing to meet Kaori's passion, she responded to the kiss in turn. Their tongues intertwined, coiled together in fierce fervour. Kaori's hand continued to fondle her body. Her breath came out in fits and starts as if she was being controlled by those five fingers that were finding their way across her. The thought that this was the first time in her twenty-six years she had ever felt such passion embarrassed her, but she was intoxicated by this pulsing electricity that seemed to rise from within like a wave. She was awash in an ecstasy that threatened to make her lose consciousness, so she closed her eyes and let Kaori have her way.

However, as soon as Kaori's fingers came close to her genitals, she felt a shudder of fear ripple through her. The faded memory of that night came back vividly in her mind, and she swiped Kaori's hand away. Kaori stopped moving. "Rie?" she asked, fear in her voice.

She realized she was crying, the pillow already wet with tears. Kaori had noticed something was wrong and so sat up and turned on the light. The darkness in her heart hid itself with the light that suddenly filled the room.

"What's wrong? Are you okay?" Kaori asked, wiping away her tears.

"I'm sorry," she said, her voice full of sobs. "I'm sorry."

That was all she could say.

Kaori paused in thought for a moment before laying back down next to her and embracing her.

"It's fine. Let's stop here, okay?" she said gently. Kaori's words flicked a switch in her head and she buried her face in Kaori's chest. Her shoulders shook as she said "Thank you" over and over again in a choked voice.

Kaori continued to stay at her apartment after that night and spent the rest of the New Year's holidays until the fifth there. She decided to use her paid leave so they could share the time off together. The fifth was also her birthday, so they decided to celebrate with a cake. Kaori had bought wine, but as she wasn't so keen on its bitter, sour taste, she bought a few canned cocktails from the convenience store. The two of them clinked their glasses together, sat around the six-inch cake ready to eat on her *kotatsu* table. The pure chime of their glasses echoed, and she remembered a song she had loved as a child.

> *Let us come together, and live in this world in*
> *    our own free way*
> *Upon our steeds, we'll enjoy the glittering*
> *    world of the living*
> *So, raise a glass to one another, as we sing*
> *    songs of the joy in our hearts*

*We won't waste a moment of our youth and
we'll live with passion*

The song was from the opening of a popular drama, *My Fair Princess*, that had swept the Sinophone region when she was in elementary school. Even now she felt a yearning in her heart for the free, unrestricted lifestyle the song's lyrics illustrated. In particular, the line about raising glasses and singing together spoke to her; it was a reference to one of Cao Cao's poems: *One must sing if one has a drink in hand / Just how long are our lives? / They are like the dew / Fading days are many.* In other words, life could end at any given moment. Her drink wasn't very strong, but she felt her emotions were the same as Cao Cao's. Yet here, in this "land of mulberries," this island to the east of China, sitting around a Japanese low table with her Japanese lover, making a toast with Western glasses, here she was thinking of a Chinese poet from over eighteen hundred years ago —she couldn't help but laugh at how jumbled this mixture was.

"What's so funny?" Kaori asked.

"Nothing, just remembering something."

"And that is?"

"*So, raise a glass to one another, as we sing songs of the joy in our hearts.*"

"What are you on about? You are a strange one."

"You're not wrong. I may look normal on the outside, but I am in fact very strange."

If she had to pick someone to come together and live with, she would like it to be Kaori. The two would accept everything about each other, and in this world that felt so small and constraining yet so full of landscapes she'd never seen before, she would explore every corner with a song on her lips; one day under the spring breeze, another looking up at the autumn moon. To realize this fantasy she needed to come clean to Kaori. It was finally time to put a stop to her endless dance, alone and in the dark.

She had been keeping her eye out for an opportunity to explain what had happened on New Year's Eve, and after puzzling over a thousand different solutions, she decided that her twenty-seventh birthday would be the best time. Surely Kaori would draw her close and whisper in her ear, something like "It must have been a real ordeal, but it's okay now"; she was sure of it.

It didn't take long for her to realize this was a naive way of thinking. The last scene of *All About Lily Chou-Chou*, rented from the local Tsutaya, played out and she aimed for that silence that follows the end of a movie. "There's something I need to tell you," she prefaced, leaning against Kaori as she quietly began to lay bare her past—about the incident of that night, the dark university years that followed, about Xiaoxue leaving her, her time seeing a psychiatrist. She revived those frightful memories, and saying them out loud was more strenuous than she would have ever thought. Her voice was shaky, often catching in her throat. After what felt like hours of talking, she finally brought her story to a close. Silence filled the room once more.

"Why did you hide this from me until now?"

She doubted what she'd heard—words that were far colder than she expected, words that took a few seconds to appear as a criticism. A wave of coldness seeped over her body; her heart felt as if it was being strangled. She could only look at Kaori with surprise in her eyes as she waited for her to go on.

"You've had an experience with a man. Not only that, you're a mental case. Don't you think you should've told me about some of this stuff earlier?"

Kaori didn't raise her voice, simply laid her accusations out. Each word felt like a freezing blade of ice piercing her heart. She wasn't sure herself why she hadn't said anything earlier. Was Kaori really implying that she had to come clean about having mental health issues and that she'd been a victim of rape every time she met someone new? At any rate, she didn't currently have the ability to argue back.

"I don't tell anyone ... Kaori, I ... I couldn't ... Only if they were special enough ..."

She felt cold. Her legs, despite the warmth of the heated table, felt like they had turned to ice. She couldn't talk like she wanted to. Usually so fluent in Japanese, now some part of her brain had shut down—she couldn't form a single sentence. Her voice started to crack.

"And you don't think that this was deceptive?" Kaori spat as she pushed her away and stood up. Kaori's voice was as cold as she felt. She looked up at Kaori, and as soon as their eyes met, she seemed to lose all sense of balance, as if she were falling into an endless pit. It felt as though there was a hole in her heart, as if Kaori's disgusted look had pierced straight through her chest like an arrow.

"I can't be with you."

Kaori quickly gathered her things and headed to the front door.

"Wait ..." she finally managed to say, the effort of this one word requiring all her strength. Kaori paused for a moment. "Are you ... leaving me?" she said, her face turned to the ground. She didn't have the courage to look at Kaori, but she still felt a fiery glare burn into her.

"You're the one who was dishonest. You did this to yourself."

Kaori opened the door and left her house, and at the same time her life. She heard the door swing itself shut. Time itself seemed to stop, and the world was enveloped in a suffocating quiet. All she could hear was the pounding of her own heart. *Why is this thing still beating? Pathetic. Squirming like a fish whose head has been cut off.* Under the indifferent light of the room, she sat on the floor in stupefied silence.

# CHAPTER 12

**Thursday July 3: Clear skies followed by clouds**

Today is the day of my bimonthly hospital visit. I'm not sure if there's any point in seeing the doctor, but the old hospital ward of the National Taiwan University Hospital where the psychiatric department is located is this brick building that I can't say I dislike. The main hospital building is a relic of Japanese colonial rule and I like the pomp of its Renaissance-style design, and the old ward is so quiet you forget about the bustle around you and that from Changde Street and Zhongshan South Road outside. Whenever I come I have to wait two to three hours before being called to the examining room, but when I get out a book and read it under the not-too-bright golden sun that filters in through the window, I sometimes forget I'm a patient in a hospital. On the other side of the window is a beautiful green lawn.

**Friday August 8: Sudden thunderstorms in the afternoon**

Xiaoxue is coming. I looked online for this year's university intakes, and I saw the name *Yang Haoxue* alongside the words *National Taiwan University, School of Social Sciences*.

Xiaoxue hasn't contacted me. She could at least have told me she got in. But I can't blame her. After all that awful stuff I said, how much pain I caused her, I bet she thinks the further away from me she is the better. I know we're at the same university, but she probably doesn't want anything to do with me. Funny how her wish came true after leaving me. There was nothing good to come of being with me. Our being in love led to tragedy and ushered in destruction. Even if nothing had happened to me that night, I'm sure we would have gone our separate ways anyway. I mean, it's true—what we had was wrong.

**Thursday September 18: Clouds**

It's been four days since the start of the new school year. We can still change classes, but my timetable's already so full with required modules that I barely managed to sign up to the Chinese Literature Department's Readings from the *Songs of Chu* and Selected Contemporary Novels courses.

My appointment last week made me miss the first class on the *Songs of Chu*. There's a lot of students taking it and the first week's only the usual course-outline stuff so there's no real negatives to missing it, but for some reason I felt really anxious.

It's not just today, I've been feeling on edge recently. With the arrival of all the new freshers, the campus suddenly feels so much smaller. The canteen is always packed at lunchtime now and simply being there makes me feel like I'm going to collapse from oxygen deprivation. I feel even worse when I think that Xiaoxue is probably somewhere nearby.

**Wednesday October 1: Rain**

We were practising counting words in Japanese Conversation II today. The professor said, "All you kids are smart, so you should have lots of babies and pass on your clever genes," before pointing at each of us and asking "How many children do you want?" or "How many children are you going to have?" When I was asked, "Chō, how many children are you going to have?" I didn't know what to say and ended up not saying anything at all.

**Friday October 31: Storms**
It's been half a year since Dr Chen asked me to start writing this diary. It's a bit late coming, but reading back on it I've noticed something: I'm not the same me when I'm writing. It's as if a small crystal of rational thought is extracted from my mad soul, and this rationality creates another version of myself who puts these words on paper. Thanks to the diary, I can analyse myself logically without allowing myself to be affected by my swinging emotions. Maybe this was Dr Chen's intention all along.

Unfortunately, I can only write my diary when I'm already relatively calm. At any other time, if I'm not already spiralling into a pit of self-destructive despair, then it feels as if I'm separated from the world by a thick sheet of glass, as if nothing has anything to do with me.

### Wednesday November 5: Clouds
Again, people are talking shit about me. You don't know a fucking thing about me! You can get fucked! Go to hell!

### Friday November 7: Clouds followed by clear skies
Reading Wednesday's entry again, I finally understand how much my emotions are in flux.

During Japanese Conversation II we had to get into pairs to do some practice conversations. As usual I didn't have a partner so I sat alone reading over the conversation script. I tried to leave the classroom as quickly as I could once the lesson was over, but I had to go back because I forgot my pencil case. As I was coming back in, I heard these four girls who always hang around together talking about me. "Why does she always have that gloomy look on her face? Who the hell does she think she is?" "Just how long is she going to be wallowing in the past? Honestly." I had started running before I knew it and had written that hate-filled entry as soon as I got home.

The thing is, they're right. How long do I have to wallow like this before I'm saved? How long do I have to stay in this bottomless pit enduring this pain?

**Thursday November 20: Light rain**

I came out to Dr Chen. I'd told him about that night before but had kept quiet about the illicit relationship between me and Xiaoxue until now. The thing is, even *I* know that being a lesbian (oh, that word) is one of the central parts of this problem, so it would only have been a matter of time before Dr Chen found out.

He had asked me one day if there was something I was hiding from him as he looked right into my eyes. I said that there was nothing in particular, but obviously that didn't fool him. Dr Chen said I didn't need to tell him, but that he thought it might be a key clue in working out the cause of my "self-rejection."

I said to him, "So you're saying being ra— what happened that night—isn't the only cause?" Dr Chen replied saying that wasn't exactly what he meant. He said there might something else, something important, and asked me to think about it, "for my own sake."

I didn't have to. I knew full well. I stayed in silence for I don't know how long before I told him, "I can't fall in love with anyone but women." As soon as I said this, an avalanche of memories came rushing through my brain—Danchen, Xiaoxue, the violence of that night, that man's words ...

"I see. Why do you phrase it like that?" he said. "Instead of saying you can't love anyone but women, why don't you simply say you love women?"

I wasn't sure how to respond.

**Saturday January 31: Clear skies**
I went home for a week over the Lunar New Year. On Lunar New Year's Eve, I had dinner on the veranda with a group of people who I think were mostly my relatives. They spend most of the year working in China and only

come back once a year or so. I didn't know any of their names, but they knew a lot about me and kept looking over at me while they spoke amongst themselves. My mum put on this fake laugh while talking loudly with me, so I couldn't hear their conversation.

**Monday May 11: Clear skies followed by clouds**

I was walking past the Fu Bell on campus during lunch when I saw something strange that made me stop in my tracks. Around the Fu Bell and the fountains in front of the Administration Building, hundreds of students were gathered. A lot of the students had dropped their bikes nearby, and a number of them were waving the school flag. I pricked my ears and heard them chanting slogans like, "One hundred huge reforms! Ten thousand hearts as one! Taida forever!" Their shouts of "reforms" felt good on my ears, so I spent a short while watching.

Then all of a sudden, in the middle of that gorgeous spring day, I spotted someone in the crowd, her hair tied up in a ponytail, chanting along with everyone else—it was

Xiaoxue. It felt like all the sounds in the world pulled away like the tide, as if it were only me and Xiaoxue left. At that moment I knew: Xiaoxue had also noticed me. Her eyes had fallen upon me. Her gaze burned through me, hundreds of times hotter than the heat of the crowd. I averted my eyes immediately, and left the square. A part of me hoped Xiaoxue would chase after me, but it didn't take long to realize this was a desire solely on my part.

**Thursday July 9: Storms**

"You didn't do anything wrong, Zhao. You need to stop blaming yourself."

How many times had Dr Chen told me this by now?

If his story were true, if I really had done nothing wrong, then why did it hurt this much?

I once thought the same thing: I didn't do anything wrong, it was all that man's fault. But after all those rumours, all the made-up stories that were told behind my back, I began to feel that it really was me who was in the wrong.

When I told this to Dr Chen, he said that it's been a year and a half since starting treatment and he thinks we've made great progress. He then said that I should rest up over the summer holidays, and during the new semester I should be brave and "take the first step towards something new."

My mind was fuzzy and I couldn't find the words to reply, but I felt the kindness in his support so I nodded that I would try.

### Monday August 10: Rain

After reading Lin Wenyue's *One Year in Kyoto*, I suddenly feel this huge urge to go there.

Wenyue used to be a professor in Taida's Chinese Literature department and translated *The Tale of Genji* into Chinese. She wrote *One Year in Kyoto* in 1969 when she spent a year studying at Kyoto University, and here I am now reading the 2007 reprint. There's a gap of forty years between this edition and the time she originally went to Kyoto, and that thirty-six-year-old woman is now almost eighty. Apparently, the friends she made in Kyoto passed away not long after the turn of the century. The letters of condolence

she sent remained unread; they were returned, addressee unknown. Time devours
all, all but words.

There's no time like the present. I've made
sure my passport's still in date and have
already begun planning my trip.

**Wednesday August 19: Good weather**
The hottest days here in Kyoto don't have the
stifling humidity of Taiwan, so the sunlight
over the city feels really nice to me. I might
have chosen a boring time to come, without
the city being decorated in cherry blossoms,
maple leaves, or snow, but maybe that's the
reason there aren't many tourists, which I
prefer.

Walking a short distance from Ginkakuji,
I found my way to the Philosopher's Path.
Lin Wenyue lived around Shirakawa-sosui
Street four decades ago, and I wonder if she
used to watch the koi in the river on her fre-
quent walks around here. Led by the words
she left, here I am forty years later looking at
the same river she once looked at. It really is
a strange feeling.

As I let my legs carry me down the Philosopher's Path, I encountered a stone bridge called Senshinbashi—"bridge of a clean heart." As I crossed it, I saw a sign for Hōnen-in. I remembered I'd read somewhere that Jun'ichirō Tanizaki is buried at this temple, so, spurred on by this uncertain memory, I climbed up the steep road that leads there. The road is surrounded by woodland, making it cooler as soon as I headed under the branches. After a bit of walking, the temple gate and a stone relief engraved with *Enter not with garlic and wine in hand* came into view. Opposite was the graveyard, filled with gravestones standing tall like trees. No one was around, just the air awash with the cries of cicadas. As I walked around the cemetery, I found the two stones I had been expecting to find. Upon one was the character for emptiness, the other loneliness, and upon both were engraved the words *By Jun'ichirō.* I stared vacantly at these stones for a while. To think that an author, who lived to the grand age of 79, would choose these two characters as a footnote to his life, made me feel empty, alone.

I continued my walk around Hōnen-in and

soon came across a Jorō spider, sitting in the middle of a huge web. Nearby, a different spider, a dull thing the colour of a decaying leaf, was in another web—this one glowing with silver light.

### Wednesday August 26: Light rain

My week-long trip is over, and I'm back in Taipei.

The time I spent in Kyoto was amazing. I didn't worry about people looking at me, or get annoyed by the bustle of the city. Every morning was refreshing, and I was able to pass through the city with a calmness in my heart. I didn't realize how relaxing it could be to be somewhere you've never been before, free from anyone you know.

### Wednesday September 16: Clouds followed by rain

Today was the third day of the new semester. In the evening, I went to the welcome party for the Sign Language Society.

I've been thinking about what Dr Chen meant when he mentioned taking "the first step towards something new," and I think I know now. I'm sick of hiding in my shell. It's this glass shell that has distanced me from the world, protecting me from it. If I avoid interacting with people more than I need to, then I can avoid getting hurt more than I need to as well. But … if the outside world has a place for me, then I want to try going out there to find it.

So I've decided to at least head to this club. Taida has the most clubs and societies of all the universities in Taiwan, so I'm sure there must be a place for me somewhere here. I was scared I might bump into people from my course—or Xiaoxue—so I pondered long and hard about what club to join and after a lot of consideration decided that it would be the Sign Language Society. If I learn a new language, one without sounds, then my own world will grow wider. It's quite an appealing idea. Not only that, I doubt my course-mates, more focused on pop idol and visual kei groups like Johnny's, would be interested in joining.

The welcome party was held in a room in the multifunction building. We spent the first part of the event eating snacks and watching the senior members of the society (though I'm older than some of them) perform a song in sign language, before learning from the teacher how to introduce ourselves. The teacher is hard of hearing and I had some difficulties working out exactly what he was saying, but he's a really friendly guy in his late thirties. It was mostly freshers among the newcomers, but there were a few other third-year students aside from myself. Fortunately, none of my peers on the Japanese Lit course were there. I feel as if I may be able to forge some human relationships here, somehow. As this thought came to me, my chest filled with a rush of hope.

**Saturday October 31: Clear skies**
This happened during the night. I was browsing the PTT forum, checking out some posts online, when I saw a photo from Pride.

I was aware the annual Taiwan Pride Parade was today. I also imagined that Xiaoxue would definitely be there. Even so, when I saw her in that photo, I couldn't help but feel a rush of sorrow. She was walking in the parade with other people who help at the Taiwan Tongzhi Hotline, with a rainbow flag in her left hand, and her right hand holding the hand of another girl around her age. I've known for a while that she volunteers at the LGBT hotline in an educational role. Well, I found out when I saw an ad for the hotline online and saw the name *Xiaoxue* right there. I can still remember thinking *That nickname used to be mine and mine alone, yet here it is being used on an ad campaign* and how down I felt afterwards.

Was the girl walking by her side her new girlfriend? It's weird, I didn't feel any jealousy when I saw that photo. I mean, the logical, despondent part of my thinking told me it's not so unnatural for her to have found a new girlfriend a year and a half after we'd broken up. While I was bound by my memories of the incident, the world kept on turning, time kept on flowing. The world has moved on, and I'm the only one standing still.

I don't think the me of a year and a half ago would've been okay right now. I guess this is proof my mental state is slowly getting better. Dr Chen did say that my treatment was having a positive effect. And I've managed to make some friends in the Sign Language Society, and even had some normal conversations. If things keep going well in this way, I think one day I'll be free from the shackles of my past.

### Thursday November 12: Clouds

I tried to write a story for the first time in a while, but it didn't go so well. I couldn't find the right words, I couldn't think of a decent plot.

I told Dr Chen about this, and when he said, "What did you use to write about?" I didn't know how to answer. What kind of stories *had* I written? When I look at my old manuscripts, I knew that each word, each phrase, all these stories were written by my hand, but they feel so distant. The time I spent writing them feels like ancient history, the memories of writing them are faded. Not only that, stories, writing in itself, aren't simple enough to be able to respond to a question like that with a concrete answer. I thought for a moment before telling him, "They were stories about death." It seemed like an extremely boring answer to me, but he appeared to think otherwise.

He asked me why I decided to write those kinds of stories. I was again stuck for an answer, so he asked what writing is to me.

"A discussion with myself. A way to probe at the depths of my heart." I answered immediately this time.

When he asked "Anything else?" I said "Self-expression."

I couldn't do either of these things anymore, and Dr Chen was aware of that. He then asked if I'd been able to write my diary, to which I said yes, almost every day.

"But not stories. I see. Do you think there's something that you're afraid of?"

Am I afraid of something? If I had pursued that thought, I would have easily come to a conclusion. No one reads my diary, so I don't have to worry about what anyone will think. But stories are different. They're written to be read—even if you're alone during the writing process, eventually another pair of eyes is supposed to see it. I couldn't face that inevitability. In short, I'm scared to lay bare my true feelings for anyone else to read.

"The fact that you worry so much about

not being able to write shows how important this process is for you. One day, when your wounds have healed, I am sure you will be able to write again," Dr Chen said.

When I asked him when, Dr Chen had an uncharacteristically difficult expression. He said he didn't know. He stood up and gazed out the window and told me, "Though I don't know when, I am sure that the day will come. So, let's head towards it in our own time."

### Wednesday November 25: Cold, rain

I was reading Yu Hua's *To Live*, and suddenly the words "I want to live!" popped into my mind. When one door closes, another opens. If I keep this thought in my heart, I will be able to keep living.

### Friday January 1: Clear skies

I went to the New Year's party at Taiwan 101 last night with Xiaozhu, Wanrong, and Chengjie, my friends from the Sign Language Society. We arrived at the public square at seven o'clock and it was already a sea of people. We just about managed to secure a spot where we could see the stage and stayed standing there for the next five hours. As midnight approached, people began to shout out the countdown. When everyone finally yelled "Happy New Year," Taipei 101 erupted with dazzling fireworks. As they exploded in the night sky, my memories of last New Year's came back to me: I didn't go anywhere and spent the change of the year sick in bed.

After the fireworks show, due to the masses of people trying to leave, we couldn't get on the bus or the metro, so we decided to walk to Chengjie's dorm room at Taida. It took an hour and a half, but as we were talking while we walked it felt much shorter. Chengjie's roommates weren't in, so we had the whole room to ourselves and spent the next few hours eating snacks, playing card games, and practising some signs. It was super fun, but at about 4 a.m., tiredness began to set in, so we laid out some foam matting and tried to get some sleep, all four of us packed together on the floor like sardines.

This is what they must mean when they talk about "uni life." I could never have imagined I would be able to do this back during my first two years here.

Right, now I just need to get through the wave of essay deadlines and end-of-semester tests next week.

### Tuesday January 5: Clouds

After my Basic Japanese Linguistics class, I got a phone call from Xiaozhu. When I arrived at the empty classroom she'd told me to come to, suddenly she, Wanrong, Chengjie, and about ten other people from the Sign Language Society burst out of nowhere singing "Happy Birthday." Xiaozhu gave me a present and card on behalf of everyone. I had an inkling on the way that it might be a birthday surprise, but I didn't think it would be as grand as that. I couldn't help but start to cry. I was purely and simply ... happy.

### Thursday January 14: Rain

As soon as my last exam finished, I rushed out of uni and headed to the hospital.

I told Dr Chen about my new friends and he gave a beaming smile. Encouraged by his expression, I asked without thinking, "So, do you think I'll make a full recovery soon?"

Dr Chen avoided the question with one of his own: "What do you think it means to make a full recovery?" I didn't know how to reply, so Dr Chen soon went on, "Why don't you treat this question as homework? Consider what a full recovery means to how you feel. Imagine that day, not so far off now, where you will finish your therapy, and think about it, okay?"

### Friday January 22: Clouds

What does it mean to make a full recovery ... I can't put it into words, let alone get my thoughts together. I doubt it's as simple as "Living a normal existence just like anyone else," it needs to touch on something internal, something in one's mental state. At any rate, I know I can't make the indulgent wish to return to how I was before the incident, either physically or mentally. That night is a brand on my skin that I must bear for the rest of my life. It is impossible to ever erase it.

### Sunday January 31: Rain

I've just come back to Taiwan from the Sign Language Society's four-day winter retreat.

They apparently have a trip twice a year—once in the winter and once in the summer—but this time it was co-run with the Sign Language Society at National Tsing Hua University and held in Hsinchu. We stayed for three nights and four days, and the programme was jam-packed—including games, intensive lectures, plays, songs, and performances in sign language, as well as mingle sessions with high school students from a school for the hearing impaired.

"Are you having fun, Yingmei?" Xiaozhu asked me out of the blue on the second night, during one of our free periods. We were sitting by the campfire, warming our bodies from the chill of the wind while we watched the others dancing and chatting around us.

When I told Xiaozhu I was, she said, "Because you often have a real lonely look in your eyes. I sometimes feel this wall between us. As if we're separated by a thick sheet of ice."

I laughed, avoiding her question, telling her she was overthinking. But still her words reverberated in my chest. I felt as if my heart were being suffocated. By a thick wall. And as long as I still feel that way, I doubt I can ever say I have fully recovered.

### Thursday March 18: Clear skies

"I think it's the ability to forget," I said to Dr Chen.

"What is?" he replied, a gentle smile on his lips.

"What it means to fully recover," I said. "I think that's the final state I need to reach. Maybe I can't erase the fact that the incident happened to me, but maybe I can heal by forgetting the wounds I endured. Or at least that's what I think."

It was only for a moment, but I saw a troubled expression flash across Dr Chen's face. His usual calm smile came back in an instant, but during the moments of silence that followed it seemed like he was searching for the best words to say. After five, maybe ten seconds, maybe longer, he finally spoke again.

"Zhao, do you think you can completely forget something?" he asked me. I told him that while it might be true that you can't forget something completely, you can at least make yourself stop remembering it.

He said that this was "one approach," but it was clear from his voice that he wasn't completely convinced, so I asked him, "What do *you* think?"

He replied slowly, considering his response. He said that "human memory is a tricky thing" and that apparently there are things you can't forget no matter how much you struggle, and that goes for the opposite, also. Dr Chen told me he thinks we shouldn't be so reliant on memories either. He paused for another moment, before going on: "'Forgetting' may be all well and good, but I want you to consider 'reconciliation' as well. Can you do that?"

**Wednesday May 26: Clouds**
It's no good. I can't continue living in such a narrow world. I've tried so hard to claim something for myself, must I lose it all again? I need to escape, go somewhere far away. This island is a living hell.

**Thursday May 27: Rain**
I decided to stay in bed and skip all my classes. When I woke up, I suddenly remem-

bered I had an appointment at the hospital, but when I hurried to look outside I noticed it was dark out already. Endless drops of rain were pounding on my window, sounding like some kind of chaotic symphony. The clock said it was already past 9 p.m.

### Saturday June 26: Sudden thunderstorms in the afternoon

With the end-of-semester exams comes the end of the school year.

The Sign Language Society had an end-of-semester party but I didn't go. I haven't been to the club for a month now. Xiaozhu tried calling me twice this afternoon, but I panicked and as I was debating about whether to pick up or not it stopped ringing.

### Thursday July 8: Sudden thunderstorms in the afternoon

I can't get the idea out of my head that I need to leave this island. I want to leave both it and the memories of my horrible past behind and start a new life somewhere where I don't know anyone.

I've been looking at entry requirements for

master's programmes in Tokyo. A metropolis of ten million people surely has a place for me. The Graduate School of Letters, Arts, and Sciences at one of the private universities in the city has good funding and is actively looking for graduate students to study Classical Chinese Literature in Japan and Comparative Chinese and Japanese Literature. I looked at previous entry-exam questions and didn't have much problem with the majority of them.

**Thursday August 19: Clear skies**
I met with Dr Chen for the first time in five months. When I told him I was going to Japan after graduation, he asked me why I had made such a "sudden" decision, so I told him about what happened with Xiaozhu and the Sign Language Society.

"Do you not think that's just running away?" he asked when I finished. I told him yes, maybe. But I would run away properly, I'd change my name. He then asked if this was part of my "process of forgetting." I told him that while you might not be able to forget the past, I at least wanted to leave it behind.

Dr Chen then brought up the comment he'd made last time I was here, about what I thought "reconciliation" would mean. I told him the conclusion I'd come to: "It's accepting the scars of the past as a part of yourself and reconciling yourself with that fact. Is that right?"

Dr Chen looked at me and said, "You're very smart, Zhao." I shook my head and told him that understanding what reconciliation might mean is different to actually following it through.

Dr Chen paused for a moment before telling me that he wouldn't stop me if this was what I really wanted. He mentioned that he thought himself that I might find some sort of turning point for myself in Japan. However, he had to let me know that even if I did manage to escape from Taiwan, I wouldn't be able to escape from my life.

"No, I don't believe that." I replied. "There *is* a way to escape from your life."

"And that way is one I cannot really support as your psychiatrist," Dr Chen had said, with a bitter smile.

### Wednesday August 25: Typhoon

The rain has been nonstop thanks to the typhoon; it's been like this for three days now.

I've thought of a new name. Seeing as I'm going to Japan, I thought it would be best to pick a name that works both in Chinese and Japanese, so I spent a while looking through kanji dictionaries and name encyclopaedias, even trying to use some name generators, and have finally settled on one. I haven't changed my surname, but my new first name works in Chinese as *Jihui*, and as *Norie* in Japanese.

### Monday August 30: Clear skies

I went to the city hall and got my name officially changed. You need to give in your student ID, so I thought it would be best to get it done before the new school year begins.

Looking at my new student ID and seeing my new name fills me with a strange feeling. Zhao Yingmei has disappeared from the world, and born anew is Zhao Jihui, is Chō Norie. I wrote my new name over and over in a notebook. I said it out loud, feeling how it sounded.

My old name, Zhao Yingmei: she who greets the plum blossoms. I like how that name sounds, I like its meaning too. In truth, I don't dislike that name, but this is my only way forward. Snow is gone from my life now, so it makes no sense for plum blossoms to remain. Come to think of it, I've never actually seen snow or plum blossoms before. They've both only ever existed in my head.

### Monday September 13: Clouds

The first day of the new year. Because fourth-year students don't have a lot of compulsory modules, today I only had my class on the *Book of Songs*. I didn't have anything to do in the afternoon, so I decided to read back through my diary, and I noticed that I hadn't written anything about what happened on the night of May 26.

It's been four months since then so I don't remember exactly how the conversation went, but that Wednesday began the same as any other with the Sign Language Society meet. We finished at around half nine, and some of us went to grab a late-night bite to eat. I was thinking of going along when Xiaozhu called me over and said she had something she wanted to talk about, suggesting we go for a walk.

It was a cool May night; walking around the campus in the cool night breeze felt good. The moon was almost full and in its glow we went along Palm Avenue, made our way up Mahogany Avenue, and came out to Sweet-gum Avenue near the back entrance of the university.

"I'm not sure if I should be saying this, but, Yingmei, I want to help you," Xiaozhu said as the lawns behind the library came into view.

I had a bad premonition of what was to come, but I chose to play dumb. I asked Xiaozhu what she could mean.

"I found out. About what happened to you," she said, staring right at me. My misgivings had hit the mark.

I asked her who had told her. I tried to keep my composure, but I could feel my voice shaking. Xiaozhu seemed unsure of what to say before telling me that everyone in the society knew. Apparently she'd found out by chance at a group lunch and didn't know who the first to hear was.

I didn't respond, and Xiaozhu, flustered, said no one was gossiping about me, but whatever she said next just washed over me. In my muddled mind, the only thing I could think of clearly was the freckled face of that girl who had approached me in our first year. That conceited fake sympathy was the thing I feared the most. I didn't think Xiaozhu was acting like that, though, and I didn't want to consider that possibility either. But did I really understand her enough to say that for sure?

"Thanks. Can I have some time to think about it on my own?" I said, or something to that effect, before I turned on my heels and headed home, Xiaozhu's stare on my back.

Why had everyone found out? Who was the one who leaked the information? Someone on my course? One of my old roommates? Someone from school? I felt there were so many possibilities that it was pointless to try and work it out, but I couldn't help ruminating. I felt paranoid—whenever I left class, I wondered if the people who sat next to me, people I didn't even know, knew about me?

Walking around uni, it was as if everyone were staring at me, belittling me. My incident had become the gossip of the university without me knowing—my mind was full of the image of people laughing behind my back.

If I stayed here any longer, these worries would eventually wear me down. Even if no one was being directly horrid to me, I couldn't rid myself of the possibility that people were speaking ill of me behind my back. Maybe it wasn't other people's malice I was scared of but rather their knowledge of the incident. Just as a soy-sauce stain on white clothing is harder to get out the wider it spreads, the more people that found out about my past, the harder it would be for me to deny that night. The fact these thoughts are so strong proves how much I wanted to refute the existence of the incident. I can't reconcile with it, I can't live with it.

## CHAPTER 13

Reading her diary again, she thought: had she managed to reconcile with the incident compared to that September day six years ago where she had written that final diary entry, trying so hard to deny it? Even though it had ended in a complete disaster, she had managed to tell Kaori about it. That was the first time she had managed to show those scars to someone else, and perhaps it would remain the last. If baring her past to someone else was an attempt at one kind of "reconciliation," then it was clear it had ended in utter failure.

Fortunately, ever since the pride parade in May, she hadn't bumped into Kaori again. The fact that they had met via the internet had meant their connection was that much easier to cut.

"We're getting married," Erika had told her one day as the first chills of winter began to set in.

Unlike her and Kaori, Erika and Okabe hadn't cut their ties; they were deepening them. After the success of their visit to Okabe's parents', they had headed up to Erika's parents' house in Hokkaidō during Obon. This trip had gone well, and they married two months later in October, with a party involving both of their families following in November. The public wedding ceremony would be held in March, and Erika had invited her to the reception.

Looking at the invite, an uncertainty crept into her heart. Even the snow-white RSVP seemed to exude the fragrance of joy. Erika's face had been the image of happiness when she'd handed over the envelope. Was she really allowed to come, to be present at this union of pure, unadulterated bliss?

Her phone began to ring, pulling her out of her thoughts.

"Hello? Xiaohui?" There was none of Sho's usual easygoingness from the voice that came out of the phone speaker. "Can you come? Now?"

She looked up at the clock on the wall. It was already past 10 p.m.

It took her thirty minutes to reach Ogikubo Station, and it would take another fifteen to walk from there to Sho's house. Sho was waiting at the station and was clearly scared of something, her eyes darting around.

"Seems she hasn't followed us here," she said, looking around the station exit; past 11 p.m., there were few people around. The woman they were referring to was Sho's ex-girlfriend, the one Sho had broken up with before coming to Japan. This ex had found out via social media about Sho's new girlfriend, Aki, and had decided to fly all the way out to Tokyo and stalk Sho. Sho wasn't one to take things seriously and didn't much care about her online privacy, and so, with all of her location-tagged social media updates, it was easy for her ex to work out where she lived and where her language school was. Sho had already confronted her many times, asking for the stalking to stop, but it hadn't made a difference.

"Luckily, Aki's super careful when it comes

to her own privacy, so she hasn't found her yet," Sho said. Her face was the picture of exhaustion. It was clear just by looking at Sho how much of a mental toll the stalking was taking. But Sho hadn't reached out to anyone, instead choosing to deal with it alone.

"This is happening because I didn't think about her feelings and left her to come to Japan on my own, for the sake of my own life. I can't put all the fault on her. I felt this was something I needed to fix by myself."

However, the stalking had reached a breaking point. Three days ago, December 1, was Sho's birthday, and so she and Aki had taken it as an excuse to spend three nights in Shizuoka. Earlier today, when Sho had arrived back in Tokyo from the holiday, she opened up her mailbox to find a bloodstained letter, a bundle of hair, and the end of a finger. The letter read: *Happy Birthday. Here's my present for you.* Unsurprisingly this had unnerved Sho and she had called for help immediately.

They walked through a number of dark streets until they finally reached Sho's apartment. It was an old building, built in the early eighties, and her place on the third floor was only twenty square metres; the living room was a small tatami-matted space, and the bathroom was a simple tiled room with a metal tub set into the floor. As expected of such an old building, the apartment lacked any security measures, let alone an elevator. Anyone could come right up to her door if they wanted.

"This place really skimps on security," she said to Sho.

"I wanted to get as cheap a place as possible," Sho replied, obviously embarrassed.

"Well, you could at least close your window," she said, shutting and locking it. Exasperated, she said, "You do realize the situation you're in, right?"

She waited a moment for Sho to offer her a cushion to sit on, but upon seeing Sho slump down onto the tatami floor, she did so too.

"So, are you really going to report her? Take her to the police?" she asked.

This was the reason Sho had called her out so late. Given how complicated the situation was, Sho's Japanese was not good enough to tell the police the full extent of what was going on. On top of this, Sho's stalker being another woman was surely out of their comfort zone. Any kind of slipup in explaining the situation would cause the police to view Sho as a liar or prankster and result in her being turned away.

"Maybe not report, but I want to at least talk to the police," Sho said, her voice trailing off.

Unsurprisingly, Sho was hesitant. She sighed inwardly at Sho's continued desire to shoulder this burden alone. It took an abnormal obsession to follow someone to another country. Not only that, the fact that this stalker had seemingly put her own finger in Sho's mailbox as a "birthday present" was a clear sign that Sho was in danger.

She could understand where Sho's ex was coming from; having suddenly lost an outlet for her love, it was only natural that it would well up inside with nowhere to go—just as sediment builds in a river that cannot reach a sea. This kind of love soon transforms into a blade, set to destroy, that will indiscriminately harm anyone in its path. She too had experienced the same, and that was exactly why she knew what kind of destruction lay before the fierce wave of this now direction-less love. The only way to escape from becoming a victim of this destructive love is to cut off any old sentiments, to be as coldhearted as necessary—this was a fact she knew painfully well. Even so, perhaps Sho's inability to cut off her emotions towards someone she was once close to was one of her virtues.

"Whatever the case, you need to contact the police, right?" she said as she cast her gaze around Sho's room. This was her first time here—there was a small closet, some colourful storage cabinets containing Sho's Japanese textbooks and books on job hunting, and some simple bedding on the floor; that was all. "You've still got a picture of her, right?"

"Yeah, on here," Sho said, holding up her phone.

"Then let's get going to a police box right now. If we tell them what happened they should at least increase patrols around here," she said as she stood up to go.

The closest police box to Sho's house was

a fifteen-minute walk away. Out in the freezing night air, they pulled their arms and shoulders in to themselves. As they walked, Sho was constantly on guard, looking around her at every moment. She was intrigued at seeing Sho so on edge for the first time, but she made sure to keep her own guard up too.

When they arrived at the police box, there were two men inside who looked to be in their late thirties. She explained to them both the general situation before interpreting while they questioned Sho. Neither officer expressed much concern on hearing that Sho was a victim of stalking, yet they grew serious as soon as they saw the bloodied letter, and the hair and finger, and urged Sho to file an incident report. While Sho was initially apprehensive about doing so, when she heard that filing this report wasn't the same as a formal accusation and wouldn't result in any legal punishment for her ex, she went through with it. She interpreted Sho's verbal account and filled in the documents on her behalf.

One night, a week later, she received a call from Sho, explaining that her ex-girlfriend was at the police box and asking if she could come down. She quickly finished up her work before heading to meet Sho in Ogikubo.

The same two police officers were there, along with Sho and a woman she presumed was Sho's ex—she was in her late twenties, wearing a lilac puffer jacket and jeans. Her waist-length black hair had lost its sheen, sticking out at all angles at the ends, perhaps due to the dry Tokyo air. If you ignored the huge bags under her eyes, her well-shaped features suggested she could be quite beautiful beneath her unkempt appearance. The four of them were seated on plastic folding chairs; one of the police officers was typing away at his computer, Sho was idly playing with her phone. Sho's ex seemed anxious, her eyes darting off in every direction. One moment she would be surreptitiously staring at the police officer's back as he typed, the next she'd be looking Sho straight in the eyes. Her eyes would dart to the table upon which her dark green passport lay, then down at her hands, the little finger of the left wrapped tightly in a white bandage. Maybe her darting gaze was the reason Sho's ex was the first one to notice her arrival.

"Apologies for arriving so late," she said to the police officers, trying to ignore Sho's ex-girlfriend's surprised expression. "Sorry for keeping you, Sho," she added.

They told her that Sho had noticed her ex skulking around the area near her house on the way back from language school and had rushed to the police box. As Sho had already filed the incident report, even with her unreliable Japanese the officers had picked up on the words "girlfriend" and "stalker" and had rushed to the scene. Unsurprisingly, as neither police officer could communicate with Sho's ex, who didn't speak a lick of Japanese, Sho hadn't hesitated to phone her. The police officers didn't mind, as she was already aware of the situation.

They began questioning Sho's ex via her interpretation. This woman's name was Chen Yixuan and she had dated Sho for three years. Yixuan was against Sho's wish to come to Japan in the first place and had assumed that Sho would wake up from her "Japanese dream" after a year or so and come back to her. This belief had made her shock upon seeing Sho with a new girlfriend all the greater.

"I felt like the foundations of what allowed me to live had crumbled without a trace— I didn't know what I could rely on anymore. I felt my vision going dark. When I came to my senses, the thoughts that came into my head were that I could still stop my world collapsing—I had to stop it," Yixuan said, her eyes cast downward. "When I saw those pics of Shurou with her new girlfriend, it felt as if the fact that I'd lost her was thrust in front of me in the most vivid, irrefutable way. Losing Shurou was the same as my very world falling to pieces, so I did all I could to oppose it."

This "opposition" took the form of her coming to Japan to show Sho the extent of her love. However, as her three-month travel visa grew closer to its end date without her managing to win Sho back, she had grown desperate; an impulse led her to cut off her own finger.

Yixuan's story was full of metaphors and abstract language, so it was a struggle to interpret her words correctly. As she listened to Yixuan speak of her pain at being left behind, she couldn't help seeing herself (just after Xiaoxue had broken up with her) in Yixuan and empathizing with her.

Sho suddenly interjected: "I'm really sorry for hurting you. I know you said you were only trying to stop your own world from falling apart so that you could keep on living, but I'm not you. The only way I could keep living was by completely destroying my world and rebuilding it again. Those days in Taipei were eating me from the inside. It's like rust eating through metal—it happens so slowly that at first you don't notice it, but all of a sudden the rust has become so prevalent that there's no way to turn it back how it was. You didn't do anything wrong. We just didn't want the same things from life."

She was speechless as she listened to Sho and her uncharacteristic seriousness. Feeling her eyes, Sho returned her gaze. Then, all of a sudden: "You don't need to translate that part," Sho said, blushing.

Yixuan gave Sho a fixed stare, before asking, "Are you really not going to come back to Taiwan?"

"Who knows? If I can't get a job I guess I might, and even if I do get a job I can't say for sure I'll live out the rest of my days and be buried here," Sho began. "But whatever I choose to do, the past is the past. I can't afford to look back at it anymore. I don't know what the future holds, but right now, I want to live. What's important to me now is that I'm living here in Japan and that I have a girlfriend here. I want you to understand that."

After Sho finished, Yixuan appeared to have finally accepted the situation, and dropped her head. They didn't speak Chinese, but the two police officers had caught on that this was an important discussion, so they waited patiently.

In the end, the police officer let Yixuan off with a verbal warning and forced her to sign a written oath that she wouldn't stalk Sho again, and, with that, the questioning was over. She and Sho were getting up to leave when Yixuan's voice came from behind them: "Zhao Yingmei." She span around.

Yixuan was still sitting in her chair, staring at her. Yixuan's eyes were like endlessly deep lakes, giving off a cold, dull light. A shiver ran through her.

The police officers couldn't speak Chinese and so were understandably confused, and even Sho wasn't sure what Yixuan meant. They all looked over at her, with expressions that said: "Who?"

She remembered the look of surprise that Yixuan had given her the moment she'd arrived earlier.

On their way home, she had to ask Sho: "Did you say that Yixuan went to Soochow University with you, Xiaoshu?"

"Yeah. Same school year." Sho herself seemed relieved and was walking with a spring in her step, a carefree smile on her face. "Wait, we're the same age too, aren't we? Which means you're also the same age as her, Xiaohui."

"Do you remember what high school she went to?"

"Yes. She went to Taichung Girls' Senior High School. I wanted to see her in that green uniform so I got her to put it on for me once."

A flash of white light seared through her head, her chest felt tight. She couldn't say a

single word. Sho didn't notice her bewilder-
ment and kept on walking, whistling a tune
into the cold air.

## CHAPTER 14

Yixuan knew her. Not as Zhao Jihui, but as Zhao Yingmei.

Every time she thought of this, she couldn't sit or stand still. It was as if her chest was full of a large clump of something, making it hard to breathe.

Did Yixuan hate her? She pondered on Yixuan's cold stare again and again, looking to see what emotions were hidden within its unfathomable depths. The Chinese idiom meaning *all thoughts will one day return to ash* seemed like the only way to describe how Yixuan had looked at her—those were the eyes of someone who was devoid of all hope.

Time kept marching forward despite her formless unease, and work grew busier as the end of the year approached. Somehow, she managed to get through the hectic end-of-year period, and the relief that came with her few days off after New Year's Day was enough to make her forget about her earlier unease.

It occurred three weeks after the day she last saw Yixuan, the first day back at the office after the New Year's holidays. As soon as she stepped foot in the office that morning, she could tell that something was wrong. The co-workers who had arrived before her weren't paying her any attention and were busy typing or reading newspapers, but this indifference to her presence seemed excessive. Almost as if they were actively trying not to have noticed her appearance.

"Good morning," she said, like she did every day. It was only then that her coworkers finally looked over and answered in turn. The tone and volume of their voices was no different to normal, but she could sense that something small, something minute, was different. To use a metaphor, it was a small change in the smell of the air, the way the sunlight fell, the way the dust motes were floating around. It was something difficult to notice, a change that couldn't be put into words, yet it was enough to get her feeling anxious. Trying to suppress the rapid beating of her heart this ill omen caused, she went to her seat and turned on her computer as usual.

The reason for the strange atmosphere was revealed that evening. While she was finishing up her work and getting ready to leave, Erika, who had been with a client all day, called her over. She didn't fail to notice Okabe glancing over as Erika did so.

"What's up?" she asked, when the two of them were finally alone in an empty meeting room.

"Norie, I felt I needed to tell you … Well, I suppose you might know by now," Erika said before pulling out her phone and opening up a social media app and showing her the screen. "I received this last night."

She took the phone from Erika and peered at the screen. It was Erika's message inbox.

Chō Norie's real name is Zhao Yingmei.
She is a lesbian. She was with a girlfriend
in the high school.

After graduating high school, she has been
raped.
She had severe depression and came back
from seeing a psychiatrist.
Don't be fooled by the look of her elite.

She heard the sound of her world cracking in two. A sharp snap, like the sound of ice cubes dropped into boiling water. It didn't matter that this message looked like it was written using automatic translation software; the relevant information was painfully clear. Those mechanical words robbed her body of weight, plunging her into a sudden free fall. Her vision blurred, a ringing sounded in her ears. She almost forgot how to breathe, the pain was so terrible.

However, strangely enough, separate to her free-falling self, there was again that rational version of herself looking down upon the whole affair, coolly analysing the situation. Although the sender's account lacked any identifying information and was obviously a throwaway profile made explicitly for the purpose of sending this message, the fact that they knew about her high school life, along with the fact that they couldn't speak Japanese and had to rely on machine translation, meant that it was probably safe to conclude that this was Yixuan's work. Most likely, Yixuan had heard her current name during the police questioning and used that to locate her social media profile. Then all she had to do was translate her message into Japanese and indiscriminately send it to all her connections with Japanese-sounding names.

"And Okabe, too?" she asked. She tried to put on an air of calm and keep her voice steady so Erika wouldn't notice the level of her distress. But even so, this simple sentence seemed to catch in her throat. Any further sounds felt like they would tear through her vocal cords.

"Yeah, Takeshi got the same message," Erika said, her expression one of concern. Ever since Erika had announced their marriage, she was comfortable with using Okabe's first name around her. "I asked him to delete it, but apparently it was sent to Yuka too. She rang me last night to ask if I'd received it."

Who else had received this message? She

wanted to ask, but her voice wouldn't come out. It seemed her guess was right. It would be safe to assume all her connections with Japanese names had been sent it. This meant not only the coworkers in her division, but other friends in the office, and her other LGBT friends—details of her past had reached them all.

She cast her mind back to the strange atmosphere this morning and to Okabe's earlier stare. Knowing the situation now, she presumed that they probably weren't looking down on her. They didn't even know if the message they had received was true or not and were most likely unable to act naturally after receiving this sudden and strange information.

Fear rose up through her entire body. The fear that the incident had become idle gossip without her knowing, that people were talking about her behind her back. The fear of being driven out of a place she had carved out for herself. Each fear was like a wild beast that had been lurking in the darkness since an ancient time, reawakening with gleaming eyes, sharpening its fangs, ready to tear her apart at any moment.

"I can't believe someone would spread such baseless rumours. What kind of awful person would do that?" Erika said, as if she couldn't bear the silence any longer. "I think this fully constitutes defamation."

She was taken aback by Erika's words. *How can I tell Erika that those hate-filled sentences contain no trace of a lie?* Those five lines, the simple truth, had managed to drive the world she had built up over these past few years to near collapse. It seemed her life *was* this fragile, after all. Even if Yixuan were charged with defamation, that wouldn't change a thing.

"Thank you for telling me," she said. Then, after a pause, "You're a good person, Erika. I hope happiness awaits you." Her voice was cracking. On hearing its desperation and desolate tone, all she could do was take another breath.

For the next week, she didn't step out of her house.

She had taken the first three days off work, but with no change in her mental state, she chose not to go back. She couldn't bear the outside light filtering in, so she kept her curtains shut, rendering the room so dark her hands were impossible to see. Squatting there in her apartment, she felt as if she were dissolving into the darkness itself.

Her phone rang dozens of times over the course of the week, but she didn't answer a single call. A few of her friends contacted her through social media. "If you want to go ahead and file a lawsuit, you can talk to me," one of her lawyer friends in her LGBT circle said. "I've located the sender's location via their IP address," another friend said, a computer science student. "Was that message true?" said a lot of messages from friends who wanted to verify the credibility of the claim. It wasn't just her Japanese friends, her Taiwanese friends reached out, too. It seemed that the message wasn't sent solely to her Japanese contacts. She read the messages but couldn't find the energy to reply to any of them. Before she knew it, her twenty-eighth birthday had come and gone.

For three whole days she existed only in a cycle of comatose sleep and waking. It felt as though her nervous system had been stripped from her, and neither sadness nor happiness could reach her core. She had lost the energy to even cry.

On the fourth day, her rational thoughts returned to life and began to talk to her.

—No matter how deep the wound might have been, it's been ten years now. Are you really so scared to let such old scars be known?

*There are some wounds that don't heal no matter how much time passes.*

—Knowing your past doesn't mean that they're thinking badly of you. It's not worth worrying yourself about, is it?

*It's more that it feels like my world has been knocked out of its orbit. Even if I return it to that original orbit, it won't be as it was before.*

—Well, you're the same as you were during university, then.

*Yes. I haven't changed. I can change my name, cross the ocean, learn a different language, but I am still myself. It is my being myself that alienates me from the rest of the world. The reason why living is so hard is because I am me.*

— ...

Strangely enough, she felt no ill will or anger towards Yixuan. She assumed that Yixuan, unwilling to accept her loss, needed to seek out another target of hatred as an outlet for her feelings—such madness born of despair seemed almost pitiful.

On the fifth day, a scene passed through her mind: in the middle of a blizzard, a woman is wandering without direction through a snowfield. At the same time, she noticed a thought that felt like it had always been lodged in the corner of her mind: *This occurred because it needed to occur.* If Yixuan hadn't shown up, then surely someone would have spread her past at some other time with some other motive, with some other method. No escapist drama lasted forever. The curtain had to come down at some point.

With this realization, the whole situation moved from tragedy to farce. Her entire reason for living was to wait for death— that was the conclusion she came to. Even if her past hadn't been exposed, the script of her life most definitely had something else in store for her: an accident, a disease, a natural disaster. Something huge was waiting, something she would never be able to struggle against, biding its time, staring at her, looking for its chance—as this thought passed through her mind, she realized that it resonated with the premonition she'd had since she was young, the feeling that she probably wouldn't live long. And, in truth, something had happened—the incident had continued to pursue her and had now snapped her life in two. So she needed to set out on a journey yet again. This was the only inevitability in her life.

To her, to die was to flee from life. But she didn't mind escaping from life in this way anymore. Birth was the forced gift of life, whether the person born wanted it or not. If there was no way to oppose this injustice, then surely she had the right at least to run away?

On the seventh day, she resolved to die. It didn't come about via the shock of despair, but merely from resignation and logic. Twenty-eight. She had lived two years longer than Qiu Miaojin—and that was enough. She was surprised that she didn't feel any unease. The fear that had been tormenting her all this time had disappeared without a trace. Misao Fujimura had written in his farewell poem, *Now that I stand upon the precipice / There is no unease in my breast*, and it seemed he was right.

"But if we were to die, wouldn't you want to bloom beautifully first? For a moment before dying? You know, like the thorn bird."

A voice suddenly echoed in her ears. It was something Xiaoxue had said to her, long ago.

She traced the memory and tried to remember all the words they'd said to each other on that day together, long before the incident.

"Let's both keep on living until we're seventy-year-old grannies. Then we can find a beautiful cliff and throw ourselves into the sea from it."

That oath they had made was blinding to her now, her heart hurt just remembering it. At the same time, memories had a premonition of eventual collapse about them. Perhaps the end of her life had already been foretold by that earlier golden era.

The cliff with the most beautiful view ...

She began to search online for cliffs around the world. What Xiaoxue had said was probably intended as banter between them, but she was ready to put the idea in motion. A cliff with a beautiful view but no barrier, one where she could throw herself off easily. The sea couldn't be directly below. A rock face below would be the only way to guarantee an immediate death.

A photograph caught her eye. Lincoln's Rock in Australia. A flat grey-white cliff that gave off to a sheer precipice. Not only was there no barrier, there was also an area that stuck out almost as if it were a natural diving board. In the photo, a number of tourists were sitting down and smiling at the camera. Above their heads was a clear blue sky with a few trailing clouds; below was an endless green forest—the distant horizon joined the sky and trees together. As she continued searching, she found a photograph pointing down from the cliff edge. Below was hard rock. It was midsummer in the southern hemisphere right now; under white clouds and a gorgeously blue sky, near verdant trees, bathed by the warm rays of the sun, she could die. She doubted there was a better place to end her life than this.

Lincoln's Rock was a part of the Blue Mountains, situated a few hundred kilometres west-northwest of Sydney. Sydney International Airport would be the closest airport. While reading up on Sydney, she found out that the world's biggest pride parade, Mardi Gras, was held there in early March.

Attending the world's biggest pride parade before dying the next day—surely that was a way to bloom beautifully before dying? Now that she had made the decision to kill herself, there was no need to rush. Death was no longer reserved for some indeterminate point in the future, and she felt far more relaxed knowing when she would leap into its embrace. As she thought on this, her heart grew clear, like a silent lake.

## CHAPTER 15

The day after she resolved to die, at around ten in the morning, someone came to her door. The people who showed up on the intercom screen were her direct superior and a colleague from work. She supposed that they were worried about her continued undisclosed absence from work and had come to check up from her. She didn't see any reason to leave her apartment at just this moment, so she pretended not to be in.

As soon as she had verified that they had gone, she began preparations for her trip. She decided to use the one and a half months until March as a final farewell to this world. Writing down the places she wanted to see before she died, she began planning her journey.

It was a bit strange to see herself planning

everything so calmly. As if the rational and mad parts of her mind had finally come together since the decision. The rational part, which had until now prevented her from quitting life through all those momentary impulses, this time seemed to be helping her prepare, almost as if it had finally accepted the true depth of her despair.

Flights, accommodation, and visa preparations were sorted out within a week. Over this time, her friends and colleagues would occasionally call, but, because she continued to not answer, they eventually stopped trying.

She spent the day before her departure wandering around Tokyo. Leaving her place in Shinjuku early in the morning, she wandered through Yoyogi, Shibuya, Shinagawa, Ueno, Takadanobaba—carried across and around central Tokyo. She roamed like a young wandering monk in this city she had chosen; this city where she'd thought she would one day lay her bones to rest. In the few years she had spent in Tokyo, she had made far more memories here, hidden throughout every corner of the city, than in her birthplace of Taiwan. Human memories dissolve into the city, only coming to life again through the consciousness of self. As she walked, she etched the cityscape and these memories firmly into her mind. The night in Omotesandō when she had bumped into Erika, the afternoon spent in a rainbow-coloured Yoyogi and Shibuya, each day spent commuting to the office building–filled neighbourhood in Shinagawa, the first time she had met Kaori at Ueno Station, those walks she often took during her student days on the sloping streets of Kagurazaka and Waseda ...

By the time she arrived back in Shinjuku, the sun had already set. As always, Shinjuku gleamed brighter under the cover of darkness than during the day, and the bars in Ni-chōme's dirty high-rises were welcoming queues of customers as always. Enduring the pain in her feet, she went into Lilith, sat at the counter, had a drink, then went home.

She touched down at San Francisco International Airport thirty hours later. The plane had taken off in the evening yet arrived in the morning of the same day—it was a strange feeling, almost as if she had gone back in time.

Without a particular destination in mind, she wandered the city streets, taking them in. The rush of cars near Powell Street Station wasn't as busy as at Tokyo Station but, still, a wave of nervousness passed through her and she quickened her pace and headed north to one of the piers, where she could finally merge with the other tourists and find some peace. The pleasant afternoon sky was streaked with a few wispy clouds; some seagulls stood out on the pier's fence before busily fluttering away with a squawking sound when anyone approached; a few dozen sea lions were resting on a floating pier, enjoying the sun. Before she knew it, she'd spent a good few hours staring at the creatures, wondering how it was possible that such a carefree animal could exist.

The city was made up of endless hilly streets, and although getting on the buses was fatiguing, she had grown used to it in a couple of days. On her fourth day in San Francisco she headed unperturbed to the

Golden Gate Bridge, despite the heavens opening up above her. She only realized after getting off the bus that she didn't have an umbrella, so taking the rain in her stride she headed to the water's edge to get a better look at the bridge. She remained unfazed despite the unfaltering rain that only took ten minutes to leave her drenched. The crimson bridge was bathed in a blurry spray, its distant side invisible, covered in fog.

"Wow, I thought *I* was crazy, but you're something else!"

She looked round—a white woman with blonde hair was talking to her in English. The woman was also soaked head to toe, so it was strange she hadn't noticed her.

"While alive, there are some days I want to go crazy and do things like stand by the sea and get soaked by the rain," she answered in English.

The woman let out a laugh.

"You're a funny one. You a tourist? You look like a tourist, though I've never met one who would come all the way out here just to get wet. Where'd you come from?"

*Where did she come from?* She wasn't sure

whether to say Japan or Taiwan, but thinking that this woman might not have heard of Taiwan, she plumped for Japan.

"Oh! I can speak a little Japanese," the lady said, before continuing in Japanese, "Hello. My name is Caroline. It's nice to meet you." She said "Caroline" with an American accent, sounding nothing like the Japanese rendering of her name.

"I'm Norie. It's nice to meet you too," she answered in Japanese, before returning to English: "So, how come you speak Japanese?"

"My girlfriend's Japanese; she taught me a bit," Caroline said. "She works at this Japanese restaurant in Japantown and cooks a lot of Japanese food for me. You know, like *oyakodon*, *onigiri*, that kind of stuff."

It wasn't the food that caught her attention. "You're a lesbian, then?" she asked, trying her best to hide her surprise. She refrained from saying "as well."

"Bingo!" Caroline said with a grin.

"Are you always this open about it?"

"Depends on the person. I can't tell some of my Christian friends, you know? But I don't mind. More importantly ..." Caroline said, before pointing over at the bracelet on her wrist. It was a rainbow bracelet she had bought the other day in the Castro. "... you're one, too, aren't you?"

She wasn't sure whether to shake or nod her head, but while she puzzled over what to do, her mouth had already started moving. "Yes, I'm a lesbian. Not only that, I was raped by a man." She was surprised at herself, at those self-destructive words that seemed to be almost showing off her pain. But at the same time, she felt a kind of exhibitionist thrill in laying bare her most abhorrent secret right there in the open. Maybe it was because she was far away, in this destination with which she had no connection at all.

"You poor thing," Caroline said, staring into her eyes. "So that's why your eyes look so sad. If I were to describe the inside of your heart as weather, I'd say it was like today, wouldn't you?"

"Is that why you talked to me?"

"I guess. I had this feeling that you and I were alike." Caroline turned around, putting her back to the bridge and leaning on the barrier. "I was molested by my dad when I was sixteen. When my mom found out, she was pissed off. She kicked me out and divorced him later. I left my home state of Texas behind and enrolled at a college in California. I got a grant for my tuition, but I wound up working at this IT company to make enough money to live on—almost worked myself into the grave. I was homeless for a while too, after I couldn't pay my rent."

She was unsure how best to respond to Caroline's sudden story about herself but listened to it all. Caroline's eyes mostly faced downward while she spoke, and she noticed they were a beautiful blue, like carefully polished sapphires. Caroline didn't once look back at her, continuing to talk as if performing a monologue.

"After I graduated, I put my programming skills to work and found a job down in Silicon Valley, and finally I got myself a little bit of stability. And when I was twenty-six, I fell in love. She was a girl from Japan who came over as an exchange student. It was the happiest time of my life. But she graduated last year and went back to Japan. I said we could get married so she could get her green card and we could live here in San Francisco, but she wouldn't come out to her parents. She never told them about me, it turns out.

"Then two days ago I got a call from her. Apparently, she got married to this guy her parents had picked out for her. I couldn't believe what I was hearing. *You fucking liar*, I wanted to scream. But I had to act all calm and tell her I hoped she would be happy. I thought, what the hell is the point of a thirty-year-old woman like me losing her head over someone eight years younger?"

Caroline fell silent.

She replied, "I see. So you said your girlfriend is Japanese, works in Japantown, and makes you Japanese food, but what you meant was that she *was* your girlfriend, she *worked* in Japantown, and she *used to make* you Japanese food. It's all in the past, right?"

"Yeah. Maybe. Who knows. Whatever it is, she said she was getting married, but she never said a word about breaking up with me. Isn't that fucking rich? She can just waltz off, but here I am, still trapped." Caroline looked up at the ever-raining sky and went on, her voice was emotionless, almost as if talking about someone else's experiences. "It was here that I first met her, weather same as today. She was homesick and the language barrier was getting to her, and she spent hours staring out at the bridge in the rain. Maybe the reason I said 'hey' to you was because you reminded me of her that day."

Almost as if signalling that this topic was now closed, Caroline pushed away from the barrier and turned to face her.

"I'm tired of talking. Do you want to come to my place? It's no mansion, but it's way better than here."

Caroline lived in a small, blue two-storey house in Outer Sunset. The ground floor was a dedicated garage and storage space, and the first floor was made up of two twenty-metre-squared rooms, a small kitchen, and a bathroom. The kitchen was full of cheap-looking cutlery and kitchenware that looked as if it were bought from a dollar store. One of the rooms showed no sign that someone lived there, and the closet was almost empty —just a number of T-shirts and jeans. A few Japanese books were scattered on the bed and the posters of a Japanese idol group on the wall were coming off.

After taking a shower and putting on Caroline's ex's old T-shirt and jeans, she went to Caroline's room and sat on her bed. The sound of the downpour outside roared with a satisfying tone. Caroline took a shower after her, and surrounded by the rushing water and the storm outside, she felt the reality of the place slip away. For a moment, everything around her—the bed, the window, the chair, the desk—seemed like nothing more than bodiless images. Again she was forced to realize that here she was, on a trip, hundreds of miles away from Tokyo.

As soon as Caroline appeared naked before her, she felt as if the armour encasing her heart had been torn away. Before long, it wasn't just her heart that was stripped naked, but her body too, as Caroline's hands removed her clothes. They lay down on the bed quite naturally, neither of them taking the lead. One part of her was panicking, unsure of what to do, while the other part of her was quietly excited—her own emotions in such circumstances were still a mystery to her. Her body, which she had expected would refuse Caroline's touch, was instead almost obedient to Caroline's every whim. Caroline's hair hung wet over her face, the dampness overflowing with kindness. Suddenly she opened her eyes, and Caroline's sad, blue eyes staring back brought up a nostalgic, distant memory. She closed her eyes again and gave in to that sea of gentle memories. Sweet memories, long before the incident.

"Norie, you're thinking of killing yourself, aren't you?" Caroline asked afterwards, whispering into her ear.

Taking in Caroline's electrifyingly gentle voice, she replied, "You too, right?"

"I guess we're two birds of a feather," Caroline said with a grin. "Where did you choose as your final destination?"

"Lincoln's Rock in Sydney."

"Then why are you here?"

"I'm going on a final trip. Kind of like a ritual to say goodbye to the world. After San Francisco I'm heading to New York, then on to China." She then asked, "So what about you? I can't think of a gravesite that would match those beautiful blue eyes of yours."

"New York. Near the Stonewall Inn. I suppose that place represents the beginning of our struggle in this country, you know?"

"A beginning and an end. Like the cycle of reincarnation. Very Buddhist." She looked at Caroline. "Maybe you were Asian in a previous life."

"Maybe," Caroline said with a smile. A smile filled with sadness. "So, my Asian friend, will you come to see me off? You're heading to New York too, and it's a little lonely to go through with it alone."

"When?"

"Next week today. Eleven thirty p.m."

"I don't mind, but let me ask one thing." A wickedness suddenly came over her. "Were you having sex with *me* just then?"

Caroline's expression was one of surprise for a moment, but immediately returned to its usual calm. Caroline smiled quietly as she stared at her, appearing as if she was in complete control, as if she would never falter in the face of anything. "Of course not," Caroline said. "But neither were you, right?"

The observation deck of the Empire State Building has an indoor and open-air section. Although the open-air part allows visitors to look out over Manhattan with no glass barrier in the way, the cold winter air of the eighty-sixth floor fiercely cut through her entire body. In three minutes, her hands and feet had grown numb, her fingers refusing her commands. However, the dusk sky and the view of the city lured her outside again and again into that biting cold. The indigo-blue sky was dyed with a gradually deepening crimson the further west you looked, bringing to her mind a gel candle. The east side of the city was already drowned in darkness, and the glimmers below seemed a river of light. The actual East River was now pure black, cutting off the glow of Manhattan from those of Queens and Brooklyn.

The nightscape of a large city looks the same wherever you go, she thought. Looking out from a certain height, each person's individual life seems to lose its uniqueness and appear uniform. Ignoring such landmarks as Tokyo Tower or the Chrysler Building, she'd have been hard-pressed to describe what differentiated this view from that of Tokyo. She couldn't pinpoint what was so special about the nightscape, so why was she so drawn to it, why was she so overwhelmed by its beauty?

She thought of Caroline. Today was the day. One person's death wouldn't be huge news in a city of this scale. What kind of story, what kind of emotions had led Caroline to her death—surely no one here would care one iota. Even her own life had only crossed over with Caroline's by pure chance. They had simply seen vestiges of days long gone in each other; it wasn't as if they had managed to share in each other's pain. She had her own path. And after she saw Caroline off, she would have to continue walking it alone.

She left the Empire State Building behind and headed to the Stonewall Inn. It was past 10 p.m. by the time she arrived.

Maybe it was because she was used to the narrow bars of Shinjuku Ni-chōme, but the inside of Stonewall was larger than she had expected. With enough space to house a pool table with room to spare, it was bigger than any bar she knew in Ni-chōme. The customers were mostly men. She sat at a counter seat and the bartender greeted her with a cheerful voice. She looked at the menu and without much thought chose a cocktail that seemed like one she could drink. A white man in his thirties tried talking to her, but he seemed to lose interest soon enough and went off to talk with someone else.

What method had Caroline prepared for herself? These thoughts came to her as she sipped at her sour cocktail. Caroline didn't seem the sort of person to choose a death that would grab people's attention, so maybe when she said near Stonewall, she meant some back alley nearby. This wasn't really a city where you could easily throw yourself off a building. So, poison? A gun? A knife? Whatever Caroline had chosen, she wanted her to be there at the end, so it couldn't be that gruesome a method.

While she mulled these thoughts over, eleven thirty had come and gone, and even as midnight passed, Caroline still hadn't shown up. The bar had grown livelier, as if suggesting the night was just beginning, and the atmosphere was a far cry from death. She had no phone and therefore no way to contact Caroline.

When the hour hand finally hit one o'clock, she gave up and returned to her hotel in Queens via the subway. Maybe Caroline had abandoned the plan, or changed the place, or had the time wrong—there were endless reasons for Caroline not to have shown, so she stopped trying to think about it. It was a ridiculous notion in the first place—to ask someone to see through their suicide in a city four thousand kilometres away from where they met. It was no real surprise that she had been stood up.

After getting back to her room she had a shower, and she was drying her hair with the TV on when a certain news headline caught her eye. At 10:30 p.m. there had been a major traffic accident near Pennsylvania Station. In the collision, a car had crashed onto the sidewalk killing two people in the process.

One of the names of the deceased was Caroline.

She was speechless. After a while, an inde-scribable sense of ridiculousness filled her.

Even if the outcome were the same, she couldn't help but think that there was a huge difference in choosing to end your life at the peak of your own sorrow and getting caught up in a fatal accident. Any meaning that the former might have had was so easily erased by the latter. In the end, Caroline's death no longer had any connection with her experience, her will. Or perhaps it did, in that it ended up being the biggest tragedy of all.

At three in the morning alone in her New York hotel room, she sat upon her white bed as these thoughts passed through her mind.

## CHAPTER 16

Early February. The small, grimy arrival lobby of Xi'an Xianyang International Airport was bustling with noise.

She boarded a bus, and an hour into the rattling journey, the wall surrounding the old part of the city came into view. After night fell, she stared up at the sky by the bell tower in the centre of the district and noticed tonight was a full moon. This meant that the Lunar New Year had already passed and it was time for the Lantern Festival. She had spent so long in Japan that she had almost forgotten the existence of the Lunar New Year. Befitting an ancient capital that boasted such a long history, Xi'an was lively with festivities to celebrate this equally ancient holiday. Otherworldly lamps and paper lanterns decorated Yongningmen, the south gate of the city wall, and the long queues of excited onlookers didn't so much snake along but trail like a Chinese dragon.

After Xi'an, she headed to Beijing. Heavy snow had delayed her flight by two hours, but fortunately it had also cleansed the haze hanging over the city, and she was able to visit the Great Wall, the Forbidden City, and the Daguanyuan, all capped in powder snow. On the day she visited the Great Wall, by the time she was heading back the snow had worsened. Unable to withstand the cold, she was about to head into a nearby KFC, but she noticed a woman standing alone, looking up at the wall from her position at the bottom of a tower engraved with the words *North Gate Entrance*. Surrounded by white-silver, this woman wore a light-blue scarf and a scarlet coat, and had a purple umbrella raised above her head. Her tresses of black hair, which fell like a waterfall of sumi ink, were flecked with snow. This colourful yet stoic and sorrowful scene enraptured her, and she found herself calling out: "What are you doing?"

The woman turned to face her. Her beautiful face with its well-defined features was streaked with tears.

"I'm waiting for someone," she replied in a mainland Chinese–sounding Mandarin.

"The snow's pretty heavy—if you're waiting for someone, surely it would be better to do so inside?"

The woman didn't reply, but followed her without a word into the KFC. The door had a sign on it saying *Due to heavy snow, we will be closing at 4 p.m. today.* They both ordered fries and onion soup and sat by the window looking out on the street.

"So, who are you waiting for?" she asked after warming herself up with the soup.

The woman shook her head slightly before replying, "He probably won't show up. I knew from the beginning he probably wouldn't."

The woman was Mongolian and her name, Uuriintuya, meant *light of dawn* in Mongolian. She was from Inner Mongolia, and after finishing high school she and her long-term boyfriend had left their hometown of Hohhot and enrolled in a university in Beijing. This boyfriend's birthday was February 22, and hers was two days before on the twentieth, so they would visit the Great Wall together every year on the day in between—the twenty-first.

"He always said the Great Wall was the most impressive piece of architecture in China, and so we should ask it to watch over our everlasting love."

Uuriintuya stared down as she spoke, and her black hair shone as it caught the light reflected off the snow. *Light of dawn—it really is a fitting name for her*, she thought.

All their friends and family had expected them to marry right after university, but a rift had formed between them just before they graduated. Uuriintuya's boyfriend got hooked on gambling and both of their families discovered he owed a lot of money.

"After that, my parents were fiercely against the marriage. I realized that I couldn't go through with it either. But, even so, I couldn't break things off with him. I spent a year humming and hawing until finally *he* suggested we break up. Said he didn't want to waste any more of my life. He and his family were no longer seeing eye to eye, so marriage was definitely off the table. I told him I didn't want to break up, I begged him. And so he told me to wait three years for him. In three years, if he had finally become a man worthy of standing by my side, he would come and meet me at the Great Wall on February 21."

Uuriintuya had come on her own every year on this day to the Great Wall. All to carry through a promise that had no guarantee of coming true. All to wait for a man who probably wouldn't come. This year marked three years since his promise. And he hadn't showed.

She was surprised to hear that this kind of pure love, written about only in classical literature, still existed in the twenty-first century. A couple swearing their everlasting love at the Great Wall, two lives bound together under its grandeur—yes, this was a Chinese tale of romance that anyone would want for themselves. Even she couldn't help feel a certain sentimentality as she listened to Uuriintuya's story. But such dreaming easily falls apart when reflected in the mirror of reality. They agreed to meet at the Great Wall, but they didn't specify where—the wall was so huge that they might as well have agreed not to meet at all. Narrowing down their meeting spot to here, Badaling, didn't mean too much as it was still far too wide an area. Not only that, without a meeting time, the date of February 21 was far too vague. In other words, the two of them had no chance of meeting in the first place. Their hopeless promise seemed nothing more than a ritual to help them grasp the fact that they would never be able to be together again. And yet, she was bowled over by Uuriintuya's inner strength to keep coming here year after year.

She and Uuriintuya got the train back to Beijing North Station together. Before they parted ways, she asked, "What are you going to do next year?"

Uuriintuya paused before saying, "I think I'll go again." Uuriintuya fixed her with a stare. "It's already become a yearly habit. Plus, the trip isn't just for him. We go on journeys in order to find a better version of ourselves, and each time we do we gain something new." Uuriintuya's face cracked into a smile for the first time today. "For example, this year, I met you."

Uuriintuya turned around and walked off without another word. *How beautiful she is*, she thought. She ruminated on Uuriintuya's smile, her heart full of lament. She thought of her name again as the woman faded out of sight—"light of dawn." Yes, surely Uuriintuya would be able to persevere until dawn finally broke for her and drove away the darkness.

But she was not Uuriintuya. She would no longer be in this world by February of next year. Her final trip was slowly drawing to a conclusion. This was her solo dance. And now that the dance had begun, she had to see it through to the end.

She arrived at Sydney Airport two days before Pride. She couldn't help but be taken aback a little by the group of drag queens in the arrivals lounge who were handing out flyers for Mardi Gras. What surprised her further when she got to central Sydney were the rainbow flags that adorned almost every part of the city. Supermarkets, department stores, parks, the town hall—everywhere the rainbow flags hung like Christmas decorations. Even the cash machines were dressed up in Mardi Gras cheer with an image appearing on the screen of two women kissing with a rainbow in the background.

The parade was scheduled to begin on Saturday night at seven o'clock, and steel barricades had been erected along Oxford Street more than four hours beforehand. Hawkers selling rainbow-coloured goods were walking around, people were already milling about doing their makeup and getting dressed up. The local residents had hung rainbow flags on their balconies—the whole city was quite literally dyed in a rainbow hue.

It was still hot outside, so she went inside a Hungry Jack's, ordered some chicken and chips, and went upstairs to sit by the window. The fast-food place was full of tourists who had come especially for the festival, and various languages filled the room. She let the sounds wash over her as she stared outside.

"Hi there. Are you on your own?"

A wave of surprise ran through her—a man had suddenly called out to her in Chinese. Turning around she saw what she presumed was a gay couple in the seats nearby looking at her. The man's Chinese was unmistakeably Taiwanese.

"Yes, I am," she replied. "How did you know I was Taiwanese?"

"Because I saw *that*," he said pointing at her bag. The Complex Chinese edition of Chen Xue's *Book of Evil Women* was peeking out from her unzipped backpack.

"Your clothes and bag looked Japanese, so I wasn't sure if you were Japanese or not," the other man said in the same Taiwanese accent.

"But you don't often get Japanese people travelling alone, so I thought you were most likely from Taiwan," the first man said.

"A sound deduction," she said with a smile. Upon seeing her expression, the two men were visibly relieved. One of them went on, "You're reading Chen Xue. And you're here at this time of year. So the only conclusion is ..."

"Yep, I'm a lesbian," she said. She was shocked at the frankness of her response. "Are you two together?"

"Yeah, I guess. I'm Boyan, and this is Basi," the first man said pointing at himself then at his friend. "Basi as in 'eighty-four,' because he's 184 centimetres tall. Apparently, he's been this tall since high school."

She hadn't noticed because they were all sitting down, but now that he had mentioned it, Basi was a whole half head taller than Boyan. According to Boyan, it was a very convenient height difference for kissing, which made Basi look away in embarrassment.

"Did you both come to Sydney just for Mardi Gras?" she asked.

"No, I actually came to Sydney not long after I graduated from high school. I'm currently doing my master's in Economics here," Boyan said before looking over at Basi, who went on.

"And I'm at uni in Taiwan. But I'm here at Basi's university on a study abroad. We met at the university's gay society."

"You say that, but although we met through the society, it was thanks to a gay dating app that we really got to know each other," Boyan said with a smirk. "I wanted to get with a Taiwanese guy again, so I was looking for a fuck buddy, and when we met I was like—what the hell ... it's you!"

Basi flushed again with embarrassment before gently smacking Boyan's shoulder. "Hey, now, this isn't the sort of story to tell in front of a lady," he said.

"No, no, be my guest," she said. Their cheerful teasing was infectious; she noticed that she was laughing along with them. "So, what do you think of Sydney?"

"How do I put it?" Boyan said, pausing for a while in thought. "I've been to a lot of countries, and, to me, Sydney's got the diversity of the US, the elegance of western Europe, the cleanliness and convenience of Japan, and the safety of Taiwan. It's got the best bits of a lot of different places."

"It's also easy to live here as a queer person," Basi said. "It's like, I feel this sense of relief, like there's a place for me here even though it's not my home country. I was at the most LGBT-friendly university in Taiwan, was in the gay society there too, and had a pretty fulfilling life there. But still, I had this gnawing sensation that I couldn't fit in with the world. How do I explain it … It was as if I existed in the world, and this world was spinning, and so was I. Yet the route my arcs took landed almost in another universe to those of the world—as if they had no connection at all."

"It's like two concentric circles—together

yet apart. Although it seems like one is inside the other, the circles never overlap, just endlessly orbit, never touching," Boyan said.

"Yeah, exactly. You can't be rid of either circle, nor can they be joined. They merely exist in the same space together," Basi said, happy to have found a suitable metaphor. "But in Sydney, the two circles are in line with one another. The smaller circle is connected to the larger one. It doesn't even have to be a circle. No matter what's inside the bigger circle—a triangle, a square, any shape —they are still linked."

"You say any shape, but that doesn't mean you can do *anything* you want. That's what the law is for," Boyan said with a smirk.

"Well, yeah, obviously," Basi said, smacking Boyan as they both erupted into laughter.

She couldn't exactly follow their metaphors and felt herself barely a part of the conversation, but there was something else about what they'd said that bothered her.

"You said the most LGBT-friendly university in Taiwan ... Which one did you mean?" she asked.

"National Taiwan University," Basi said, blushing again.

Of course. She too had once dreamed of going there, yet when she finally did those four years ended up being the darkest of her life—in the Rhododendron Palace. But now, all these years later, hearing the name of the university made her feel nostalgic.

In the end, she went to the parade with this endlessly smiling couple. By five o'clock, Oxford Street was already crammed with onlookers. According to Boyan, tens of thousands of people came from across the world to see the pride parade. Cries of "Happy Mardi Gras!" could be heard from each of the many beaming faces. She marvelled at how this celebratory phrase was used just as easily as "Merry Christmas."

At seven o'clock the evening sky was still bright, and the sound of a Klaxon and engines announced the grand start of the pride parade, led by a group of lesbian bikers. Seeing the parade with her own eyes, she finally felt like she understood what Basi's metaphor had meant. This was a scene you would never see at Tokyo Pride. In addition to LGBT support groups and companies, there was an alliance of different industries—labourers, doctors, firefighters, police, soldiers—in which members of the LGBT community worked, joining the parade in their work uniforms. Even police cars and fire engines were part of the parade. Of course, there were police at Tokyo's pride parade, but they were only there to keep the peace; here in Sydney they were part of the parade. She couldn't believe what she was seeing.

In addition to these workers' groups, there were groups of people from all different walks of life—people with disabilities, Jewish people, Dutch people, Irish people, Catholics, Muslims, atheists—all holding up banners with the group they were affiliated with as they passed down the street. There was another group of people consisting of LGBT couples and their children. *I see. If I'd grown up here like these kids, then maybe I would be able to believe those slogans of* Love and Peace *and* It Gets Better, *from the heart,* she thought. Basi and Boyan were at one with the atmosphere, waving to the passersby, shouting supportive words, leaping in the air, and occasionally rating the guys who made their way past: just enjoying themselves. A warmth blossomed in her heart as she watched them, along with a bittersweet sentimentalism. Couples are almost always inherently joyous creatures. They're taken over by fleeting emotions and foolishly believe in the concept of eternity. Were she and Xiaoxue once like this? It was strange to think that she too was once like them, in the same situation as them. But, unlike them, she and Xiaoxue were never able to openly reveal their relationship to the world.

She missed Xiaoxue. *Where is she now? What is she doing?*—these questions forced themselves into her head.

The parade was in full swing until eleven o'clock, and even after it had finished, many people there didn't seem tired in the least; the crowd dissipated as some headed to bars and others to clubs. After saying goodbye to Basi and Boyan, she didn't feel like going back to her hotel either. She went to a nearby bar, drank alone until 4 a.m., and walked back to her hotel.

It was almost midday by the time she woke up. She had a slight hangover, but the sky outside was clearer than yesterday. The vivid gradation of the sky, as the pure blue above turned into soft white in the distance, relaxed her heart but also threatened to bring tears to her eyes.

After eating lunch in a restaurant in The Rocks overlooking the water, she headed to the Blue Mountains. With a road map, she drove her rented car and arrived at Lincoln's Rock without much hassle two and a half hours later. The sun at 4 p.m. wasn't as strong as it was at noon, and the slight breeze blowing in from the front felt good. Maybe it was because it was a Sunday afternoon, but there were easily fewer than twenty visitors. They would probably be shocked to see a woman jump to her death right in front of their eyes. But that didn't bother her.

The view from atop the rock was even more stunning than in the photo. The endless blue above and a sea of green trees below, stretching right to the horizon. A light mist rose from the mountain range in the distance, rendering the sky a more vivid blue. Lincoln's Rock itself was made of soft sandstone, and it would be easy to engrave words into it. In fact, looking closer, there were people's names, drawings of hearts, couples under umbrellas.

She found the area that resembled a diving board and stood out upon it. Below her feet was a sheer precipice and the hard rock ground far in the distance. Other tourists were taking photos near the edge, so no one gave her a second look. She remained where she was and took in the beautiful scenery before her. Just one more step and she would fall, staining the grey rocks beneath in a vivid red.

She recalled the sights and the people she'd seen on this final trip. The hazy Golden Gate Bridge and Caroline, who had looked out at it in the pouring rain. The white-silver Great Wall, stretching for miles like a huge Chinese dragon, and Uuriintuya who gazed up at it. The rainbow-adorned parade watched by the excited Boyan and Basi. Manhattan in sleepless New York. The gaudy red neon of the Stonewall Inn. Central Park basked in the beautiful winter sunlight. The Mausoleum of the First Qin Emperor, and the Huaqinggong Relic Site, which lie under Mount Li to the south and before the Wei River to the north. The statue of Xuanzang stood in front of the Giant Wild Goose Pagoda and the men and women of all ages who danced in the square nearby. The crimson Forbidden City covered in pure white snow and the grimy *hutong* streets covered in drizzling rain. And finally Sydney. With its sky and sea so blue it took her breath away. Those holy mountains that made you almost forget the pains of existing in this world ...

She closed her eyes. The blue sky, the white clouds, the green trees, the mountains— everything was covered by darkness. All the sights she'd seen and the people she'd met were crowding inside her head. But soon they grew still, and the surface of her consciousness returned to a calm surface, free of any ripples.

As a single tear trickled down her cheek, she realized for the first time just how much she was enraptured by the beauty of this world, how much she loved it. Living may well have been suffocating, but dying would leave too many things left undone. Through this trip, standing here at the brink of death, she reconfirmed how much she loved this world.

And yet, that love didn't have enough power to save her. Her solo dance was reaching its end and she had to draw it to a close. Otherwise it would amount to nothing more than a pitiful performance.

With her eyes still closed, she took a step forward, and felt the burden of gravity disappear.

*

She is travelling through a tunnel. A long, dark tunnel.

After an indeterminate amount of time, she finally emerges into a wasteland. She still isn't able to see anything, but she knows it's a wasteland she is in.

There's a river. It's wide and fierce. Perhaps it's rushing to join the ocean. She finds herself standing in the river. But she can't feel it flowing past. It's not cold. If anything, it's warm against her skin. She almost feels a nostalgia as it passes around her. There are other people in the river. Some from her memories, some who are not. Words are floating through the air. Some in Japanese, some in Chinese. She reaches out her hand to touch them, but they scatter and disappear.

There is the sound of a snapping thread. She squints her eyes towards the source of the sound and sees a faint light. She tries to move towards it, yet her legs are heavy and do not move. Something is trapping them in place. Her head explodes in pain and she thrusts her hands to her temples.

## CHAPTER 17

The bright light woke her up, and she found herself in a warm bed.

The sides of her head were throbbing, her body was heavy and unwilling to move. The whiteness of her surroundings seemed almost too clean. She gazed up at the light hanging from the ceiling and began to feel a sickness welling up in her stomach. Dragging her gaze down from the ceiling, she noticed two shadows floating before her. Straining her eyes, she felt her vision start to clear and noticed that they weren't two shadows, but two faces rendered dark by the light shining directly behind them. She couldn't make out their features, but she heard one of the voices loud and clear.

"Yingmei ..."

That name, that voice—they were so nostalgic. She couldn't remember what country she was in, what year it was. She blinked and the mass of white and purple light irregularly swayed in and out of focus. A door opened and someone walked in and spoke to the person that had said her name in a language her ears weren't expecting. She knew she understood that language, but she didn't have the energy to comprehend it. Sleep came down like a heavy curtain.

When she regained consciousness again, the lights were off and it was dark all around. She wriggled and managed to sit up, and what assailed her was a powerful hunger and thirst—these feelings brought with them the realization that she was still alive. She looked around the room, and with the silver glow, which she assumed was moonlight, that filled the room and the light trickling from underneath the door, she could just about make out the two figures from earlier. One was lying on the sofa, the other was sitting asleep by the side of the bed, with their head resting on it.

She tried to call out, but no sound would

come. Her consciousness still hazy, she reached out a hand and stroked the face of the person at the side of her bed. Their cheek was warm, soft. As her eyes grew used to the darkness, their face came into focus. She searched for their name through the sea of memories, and as soon as she dredged it up, her heart skipped a beat.

The person finally registered her touch and awoke, rubbing her sleepy eyes. The two of them stared at each other for a moment, and almost reflexively a certain line floated into her head: "Hello there, I didn't realize you had come too."

While she still didn't know where she was, she wasn't at all surprised to see Yang Haoxue there beside her. Just like in the library on that winter's day long ago, she appeared disjointed from reality, as if she were part of a painting.

Xiaoxue got up with a start, turned on the light, and rushed outside. Xiaoxue returned after a little while with a brown-haired woman in her forties—it was this new woman's white coat that finally made her realize she was in a hospital.

After taking her pulse and blood pressure, the doctor smiled over at Xiaoxue before leaving. Not long later, another woman, who she assumed was a nurse, came in with a tray and some food—scrambled eggs, sausages, bread and butter, and some bottled water. The other woman, who had been lying on the sofa, finally woke up and quietly watched her as she took her meal. She had shoulder-length hair and round cheeks. This woman's face seemed familiar, but she couldn't remember where she'd seen her before.

When her hunger and thirst had been sated, a number of questions came to mind along with her memories. The nurse came to take the tray away and, in English, told her to get some rest. Then, the three of them were left alone again. She and Xiaoxue stared at each other as a dreadful silence filled the room like smoke.

She wasn't sure how long they stayed like this—a few seconds, a few minutes? Xiaoxue finally opened her mouth and broke the silence.

"Why?"

She understood the implication behind

the question—why had she tried to kill herself?

"I should be asking you the same thing," she said—*why did you try to stop me?*

When she had taken that step off the cliff, she had felt someone grab her from behind. That was her last memory before her consciousness was swallowed by darkness, and she was sure it must have been Xiaoxue.

"Because I didn't want you to die," Xiaoxue said. "If you died, Yingmei, I would blame myself for the rest of my life."

"Blame yourself? But why?" She wasn't sure how to react. "Why would you blame yourself if someone chose to kill themselves?"

"It's not just someone—it's because it's you," Xiaoxue said. "My memories of you have me ensnared, they have this whole time. And if I let you die, then they would stay like that forever."

She didn't reply. Just as she couldn't forget Xiaoxue, it seemed that Xiaoxue couldn't forget her either. She suddenly doubted whether she was in a dream or if this was an illusion and took in Xiaoxue's entire body again.

Even hidden by the bed as she was, she could imagine Xiaoxue's slender frame. Xiaoxue's long brown hair hung down to her chest over her dotted chiffon blouse; her face, more grown up than the one in her memories, still had that stoic beauty, and although Xiaoxue still didn't show her emotions clearly, it had a strength of presence. She glanced up at the clock on the wall—it was past 3 a.m.

"Haoxue's not lying, you know."

Unable to bear the silence any longer, the woman on the sofa interjected. She looked over at her, but still couldn't place where it was they had met before.

The woman went on, "It's not only her, I couldn't forget you either. I learnt about your deepest scars, so why did I choose to bring it up that day? I haven't stopped blaming myself for it."

The longer she looked at this woman, the more confused she became. Then suddenly, like a severed connection suddenly being repaired, she remembered who it was.

Xiaozhu. From the Sign Language Society. That's what everyone called her. It was a nickname—she didn't know Xiaozhu's real name and apparently had never asked either. If what she was hearing was correct, then along the way she had hurt Xiaozhu as well. This realization stunned her for a moment.

Xiaoxue and Xiaozhu told her how they met. Apparently they had both been volunteering at the Taiwan Tongzhi Hotline during their time at Taida but, due to being on different teams, had only met after graduating. They had started dating three years ago and had begun living together almost immediately after. Xiaoxue was now a Civics teacher in a state junior high school in Taipei, and Xiaozhu had passed the civil service exam and was now working for the government; but despite these changes they both still volunteered at the hotline. They said their reason for coming to Sydney was part of their work with the hotline, to learn about the Mardi Gras parade.

"So, Xiaozhu, you're one of us?" she asked after listening to their story.

"Yeah, I'm bi," Xiaozhu said with a nod. "When we were in the Sign Language Society, you got along well with everyone, Yingmei, but at times you had this empty expression and faraway look in your eyes, and even when you were laughing it seemed like you were almost forcing it. At least it seemed that way to me. I liked you, Yingmei, so every time I saw you like that, it made me feel so sad."

She cast her mind back. After a society meeting, Xiaozhu had invited her for a walk around campus. The cool night breeze. The soft moon floating in and out of view as the clouds drifted by. Xiaozhu's face in profile, talking about something serious.

"I heard about your past at a society lunch, completely by chance, and thought maybe I understood the root of your sorrow," Xiaozhu went on. "Looking back, I was wrong to have thought I understood. I didn't once think it was my fault that you stopped showing up to the society."

She listened to Xiaozhu, but something felt off. This woman sitting before her and speaking of the past was not an old friend she was meeting for the first time in seven years but felt rather like a stranger who knew nothing about her. The story, too, felt like it had no relation to her, as if it were about some other person she didn't know.

She hadn't realized how Xiaozhu had felt. She was busy dealing with her own issues. Calming the stormy waves of her emotions and setting out that little boat that was everyday life was as precarious a task as walking a tightrope in the dark.

Xiaozhu slumped back into the sofa once she had finished talking. She wasn't sure how to respond to Xiaozhu's emotions, emotions she had never once given a thought to. An awkward silence followed.

After what might have been a few minutes, she thought she'd found the right words to say.

"I'm sorry, Xiaozhu. I didn't have the mental energy to differentiate between people's good and bad will at the time."

Xiaozhu gave a bright smile. "No, it's my fault. The society was an important place for you, and I took it away from you. I really am sorry," she said.

"Yingmei, you are loved by many more people than you think," Xiaoxue said, after having been silent for a long time. There was no trace of rebuke, blame, or appeasement in her voice. Xiaoxue was perfectly calm, as if she was stating a simple fact and offering it up to her. "And you love far more people than you think, too."

"How can you say that?" she said, instinctively denying what Xiaoxue had said.

"I've thought this for a long time. You often put on a front of enjoying your solitude, but actually you crave connection with other people." Xiaoxue spoke slowly, considering each word as she said them. "After all, you came all the way here to give your death some meaning, didn't you? Which means you still believe in things having meaning. If you didn't, then you wouldn't have gone this far. At least I think so."

She couldn't comprehend Xiaoxue's sudden explanation and was plunged into a deeper confusion. This confusion twisted into rage as she spat at them both: "Just what the hell is this? You two show up out of nowhere, get in my way, then go on and on about all this incomprehensible shit! After disappearing out of my life for who knows how many years?"

Xiaoxue and Xiaozhu were shocked at her sudden outburst and could only stare at her in silence. Someone passed by the door outside; the sound of the trees swaying in the breeze came in through the open window.

"You're the one who disappeared, Yingmei," Xiaozhu said slowly with consideration after getting up from the sofa. "Yes, I know I wasn't brave enough to see you for a while, but when I finally resolved to get in contact with you, you had vanished almost as if into thin air."

"Sorry about that. I changed my name and left the country. Oh, and by the way, Yingmei doesn't exist anymore. I'm Jihui now. But, whatever, I guess even if I could change my name I couldn't change anything else." After this self-effacing comment, she next questioned Xiaoxue. "And why does my death mean that you have to blame yourself? Because of this 'love' you've been prattling on about? Don't you think you're being way too selfish?"

Xiaoxue and Xiaozhu exchanged a look, taking in everything she'd said. Their shared glance indicated that they didn't know she had changed her name.

"I understand, Jihui," Xiaoxue said, looking at her again. Her tone was more polite than before. "It's true that my blaming myself is a selfish emotion. But the reason behind that feeling has a much more concrete reason than just love." Xiaoxue took a deep breath before going on. "The man who raped you was arrested four and a half years ago. He was a serial rapist, often targeting women in Central Taiwan. I thought you might be at the trial, so I went. It was held in the district court near our high school. There were five victims who gave testimonies and all of them were in same-sex relationships when they were attacked. He confessed. He said that his wife had come out as a lesbian and had eloped after leaving him. He said this was his reason for attacking lesbians.

"My question was, how did he know you were a lesbian? It wasn't discussed during the trial, but I looked up the court records and apparently that night he had been stalking us after spotting us in Feng Chia University. After we parted ways at that bus stop, he decided to follow one of us. What I'm trying to say is, it was pure chance that you were his victim that night, Jihui."

The words that had come out of Xiaoxue's mouth were so unexpected she didn't know how to respond. She wasn't sure how to react to them, how to process them, how to accept them, and in her silence, Xiaoxue went on.

"After I found out, two thoughts kept circling in my mind. *Why was it you and not me?* And *I'm glad it wasn't me.* But as that second, selfish thought surfaced, I hated myself for even daring to think it. While you were at your lowest point, there I was, self-absorbed.

"That's why I came. If you had died, I would never have been able to forgive myself. I'm like you, Jihui. I just want to be freed from the shackles of the past."

Xiaoxue was perfectly calm. Despite her impassive tone, there was an ironlike resolve at the heart of her speech.

She thought back to that hot, moonless night, and tried to imagine if it had been Xiaoxue, rather than her, who had met that fate. Almost immediately, a cold shiver swept over her—this was a thought that shouldn't even be considered. *Of course I'm glad it was me*, she thought.

*But why?* a voice whispered in her head.

*Your life isn't any less valuable than Xiaoxue's. Why did it have to be you?*

As these two contradictory thoughts clashed, she realized: *Xiaoxue has been suffering from these exact same contradictory thoughts. Dying would only end up hurting Xiaoxue …*

"So, what you're saying is, it's not that I'm weak, but that all humans are weak. Is that it?" she asked in a small voice, almost begging for affirmation.

Xiaoxue looked into her eyes as she nodded. "Not only that, Jihui … but that you're already so, so strong."

Transfixed by Xiaoxue's stare, her mind conjured an image before her. A completely pitch-dark stage in the middle of night, and upon it a dancer dressed all in black. She dances there, not making a single sound. She is truly alone—without a partner, without any audience member present. She is simply dancing on her own. Her arms draw arcs before her, she spins on the axis of her leg, rotates in the thin air. No one knows how long she has been dancing, or for how long she will continue to dance; in this empty space there exists neither time nor place. And so, she must continue to dance until her life's energy has been spent.

"Why don't you come back with us to Taiwan?" Xiaozhu suggested. "We've got a spare room, don't we, Haoxue? Whether you choose to live on as Yingmei or Jihui, it doesn't matter. With the three of us there, it'll be our own little rainbow apartment! What do you say?"

A faint beam of light falls upon the stage, cutting through the darkness. It's a door, giving off a faint warmth. *Of course. Why didn't I see it before?* The dancer moves closer and clasps the handle. It was here all along, simply hiding out of sight.

"Sorry, but I'll have to turn you down," she said after a long pause, as she locked eyes with each of them one after the other. Turning to look outside, the waxing half-moon hung silently in the firmament. She reverted her gaze to the room as she gave them both a smirk.

"*The land of mulberries is there in the distance / Your home is to the east and then further east of that land*," she said, quoting Wei Zhuang's poem, a farewell to a Japanese monk. "I already have a place I belong, one I built for myself, in Japan. I don't intend to give up on it just yet."

Upon hearing this, Xiaoxue and Xiaozhu exchanged glances, relaxed smiles forming on their lips for the first time since their arrival.

Two days later, she headed to Sydney Airport to see Xiaoxue and Xiaozhu off. She herself was due to return to Japan in three days on the return flight she had never intended to use—originally purchased so as not to arouse any suspicion from immigration.

At 3 p.m. the airport was full of travellers milling around. Whereas the majority wore outfits suited to the summer heat, Xiaoxue and Xiaozhu were carrying their jackets in their arms. What was waiting for them on the other side of that ten-hour flight was the cooler northern hemisphere and their daily lives on the small island they called home. To think that a few thousand miles could change the seasons was a funny thing.

In the end, her life went on. She wasn't sure if she would one day feel gratitude or contempt towards Xiaoxue and Xiaozhu's unexpected appearance. As they disappeared beneath the departure gate, she considered fate and its mysterious nature—if she was merely a puppet whose life was controlled by some unknown force, then was her survival due to the puppeteer's will, or the result of a rebellious intervention? Unfortunately, she didn't have the answer.

What she did know was that innumerable problems awaited her in Japan. The job she had run out on had no doubt terminated her contract by now; the rent she hadn't paid for months had probably led to her eviction from her home. All the relationships that had been torn up by the revelation of her secret needed tending to; she had to think of a suitable reply to all her friends' unanswered messages. And what about Sho? What should she say to her?

She needed to reorganize her thoughts and feelings. If she wanted to properly confront reality, there was no point mulling over possibilities and maybes.

She stared out the back window of the shuttle bus carrying her away from the airport, and the only thought that crossed her mind was the desire to write again for the first time in a decade. She felt she could write a story now, finally, after all this time.

Lai Hsiang-yin wrote: *There is nothing writing cannot cure. As soon as one is almost well, one becomes able to write—writing is the deep breath before full recovery.* And so, she must write. The story of a solo dancer, alone in the dark.

When she returned to town, it was past 5 p.m. The trees of Hyde Park were aglow in the light of the setting sun, and in their shade several families were enjoying the evening with picnics spread before them. Nearby, a twenty-year-old man was engaged in a match of giant chess with a seventy-year-old opponent, as a group of curious on-lookers observed.

Suddenly, as if feeling a gentle gust of wind rise within her, she turned her eyes up to the sky.

The sky was still bright, and soft white clouds hovered in the air.

**ARTHUR REIJI MORRIS** is a translator of Japanese literature, manga, and video games. Born in London, he graduated from the University of Leeds in 2015, before moving to Tokyo. When he's not translating, Arthur enjoys writing music and practicing Japanese calligraphy. He returned to the UK in 2019, and is now based in London.

## On the Design

As book design is an integral part of the reading experience, we would like to acknowledge the work of those who shaped the form in which the story is housed.

Tessa van der Waals (Netherlands) is responsible for the cover design, cover typography, and art direction of all World Editions books. She works in the internationally renowned tradition of Dutch Design. Her bright and powerful visual aesthetic maintains a harmony between image and typography and captures the unique atmosphere of each book. She works closely with internationally celebrated photographers, artists, and letter designers. Her work has frequently been awarded prizes for Best Dutch Book Design.

The drawing on the cover was created by Dutch illustrator Peter ter Mors, who has a special fondness for sketching birds. It represents a thorn bird, an animal whose male and female individuals look the same. There is a legend about the thorn bird, saying that it sings only once in its lifetime: after leaving its nest, it searches for a bush with long, sharp thorns, upon which it then impales itself and begins to sing beautifully, before drawing its last breath. In Kotomi's novel the thorn bird figures as a symbol for passion, art, and death. The fonts used on the cover are Miso and Big Noodle Titling, designed by Mårten Nettelbladt and James Arboghast respectively.

Suzan Beijer (Netherlands) is responsible for the typography and careful interior book design of all World Editions titles.

The text on the inside covers and the press quotes are set in Circular, designed by Laurenz Brunner (Switzerland) and published by Swiss type foundry Lineto.

All World Editions books are set in the typeface Dolly, specifically designed for book typography. Dolly creates a warm page image perfect for an enjoyable reading experience. This typeface is designed by Underware, a European collective formed by Bas Jacobs (Netherlands), Akiem Helmling (Germany), and Sami Kortemäki (Finland). Underware are also the creators of the World Editions logo, which meets the design requirement that "a strong shape can always be drawn with a toe in the sand."